Drawing Fire . . .

Kathy heard the gunfire, and her heart leaped into her throat.

"Hold on, honey!" she said.

"They're shooting at us!" Emily screamed. Her grip on Kathy's waist tightened.

Kathy didn't know what to do, and the horse started to panic.

She froze.

Clint was inside city hall when he heard the shots.

"Damn it!" he swore.

He rushed to the front doors and swung them open. As he stepped out, he saw four men at one end of the street, carrying guns. At the other end, Kathy and Emily were on their horse. He was closer to them than he was to the four gunmen, so he made a snap decision.

He stepped out into the street, drew his gun, and shouted, "Kathy! Here!"

Kathy saw Clint, saw the open front doors of city hall, and knew what she had to do. She wheeled the horse around and kicked it with her heels.

Steve Harwick saw the man come out of city hall and step into the street.

"That's gotta be Adams," he called out. "Get 'im!"

The four of them turned their attention—and their guns—toward him.

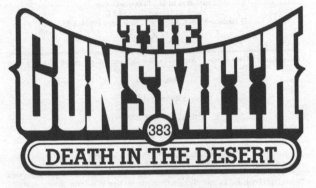

THE GUNSMITH
383
DEATH IN THE DESERT

J. R. ROBERTS

JOVE BOOKS, NEW YORK

THE BERKLEY PUBLISHING GROUP
Published by the Penguin Group
Penguin Group (USA) LLC
375 Hudson Street, New York, New York 10014, USA

USA • Canada • UK • Ireland • Australia • New Zealand • India • South Africa • China

penguin.com.

A Penguin Random House Company

DEATH IN THE DESERT

A Jove Book / published by arrangement with the author

For information, address: The Berkley Publishing Group,
a division of Penguin Group (USA),
375 Hudson Street, New York, New York 10014.

ISBN: 978-0-515-15391-0

PUBLISHING HISTORY
Jove mass-market edition / November 2013

PRINTED IN THE UNITED STATES OF AMERICA

10 9 8 7 6 5 4 3 2 1

Cover illustration by Sergio Giovine.

ONE

The smell of death.

There was nothing quite like it.

Especially for a man like Clint Adams, who had smelled it many times before.

It came to him on the wind even before he rode within sight of the town of Medicine Bow, Arizona. He'd spotted a signpost for the town a few miles back, decided it was a likely place to stop for a beer and a meal, and a few supplies, before moving on. He wasn't going anywhere in particular, just sort of drifting, spending some time alone. He'd recently stayed in a town with a lot of men and guns, and he needed to be by himself.

But as he spotted the town, the smell of death drifted to him on the air. It was unmistakable. Even his horse, Eclipse, smelled it and shook his head in distaste.

"Easy, boy," Clint said, patting the big Darley Arabian's neck, "I smell it, too. We'll have to take a look-see, though."

He continued on the road into Medicine Bow, rode slowly and carefully down the main street, which was empty. In fact, there was an eerie, empty feeling to the place that you felt in many ghost towns, but the street and the buildings did not have the deserted look that ghost towns had. In fact, several of the buildings seemed to have recently been painted. Yet there was nobody on the street, nobody walking the boardwalks, and no sounds coming from any of the buildings.

He spotted a saloon and decided to take a look inside.

He steered Eclipse that way, dismounted, and spent a few seconds holding the gelding's head and speaking to him in soothing tones.

"Easy, take it easy, boy," he said. "I'll check this place and we'll move on."

The horse nickered uneasily, but remained where he was as Clint mounted the boardwalk and approached the saloon doors.

He went through the batwing doors slowly, but there was no need. There was no one inside the saloon. Some of the tables had partially finished drinks on them—glasses of beer and whiskey, unfinished whiskey bottles—as if everyone had left in a hurry.

He walked to the bar, also found half-full drinking glasses there.

"Hello!" he called out.

No answer.

Clint leaned over to look behind the bar, then walked around to take a better look. There was nothing there. Nobody and nothing, except for lots of dirty glasses and empty whiskey bottles.

"What the hell . . ." he said to himself.

He went to the back room behind the bar, found nothing but supplies. In the rear of the saloon was a door that led to an office. He opened it, stepped inside. A desk, some filing cabinets. On the desk was a half a bottle of whiskey and a shot glass.

He went back to the bar, got behind it, and drew himself a beer. He sipped it, found it cold. Just the presence of beer told him it wasn't a ghost town, but the fact that the beer was still cold meant people had been there quite recently.

He carried the beer mug with him and climbed the stairs to the second floor.

In the upstairs hallway he saw six doors, so numbered. The first four he tried yielded nothing. The beds were unmade, and there were articles of clothing lying about, but nothing in the closet or the dresser drawers. It was as if someone had packed in a hurry.

He left the fourth room and walked to the fifth. He stopped in front of the door, took a healthy swig from the mug to finish the beer, and then tossed the glass aside. It struck the floor and bounced, but did not shatter. He had a bad feeling about the last two rooms.

He opened the door of Room 5 and walked in.

The smell hit him first. Then he realized that he had already been smelling it. On the trail, on the street, in the saloon, and in the hall. In this room, it was stronger still, because this was where it was coming from.

He walked in and looked at the bed. At first sight the man looked like he was sleeping, with the sheet and blanket pulled up to his chin. But as Clint moved closer, he could see from the paleness of his skin that he was dead. He lifted the sheet just enough to look underneath. The man was naked, and there were no wounds. That was what he had been after, the wounds that had killed him. But there were none. So with no wounds, what had the man died of? His skin was bluish and dry looking. His eyes were closed, so Clint left them that way, even as curious as he was to see what was underneath the eyelids.

Also, as bad as the body smelled in the room, this one single corpse could not be sending out the smell of death as far as the trail.

Not by itself.

And not with all the windows closed.

He left the room and walked down the hall to Room 6.

TWO

In Room 6, he found a dead woman and child. Like the man, they were lying in bed. The woman was naked, but the child—a girl of about three—was wearing a nightgown. Like the man, they had no wounds.

Clint backed out of the room quickly, and made his way down to the bar. He got a bottle of the cheapest whiskey in the house, took off his shirt, and washed his hands and arms with the rotgut. All he could figure was that these people had died of some disease. He could only hope he didn't contract it. He hadn't touched them, but he'd touched the sheets, and he'd breathed the air.

He put his shirt back on and left the saloon. His first thought was to ride out of town, but wherever he went, he might be bringing an epidemic with him. So he decided to stay where he was, check the town out a little more thoroughly.

He tried the livery next.

He left Eclipse outside the stable and went inside. He found two dead men—a young man lying in a stall and an older man in an office. Like the others, they had no wound, the same kind of pallor.

He moved on. And at each stop, more puzzling finds.

He found a dead man in the hardware store, a dead woman in some rooms above a dress shop, three dead men in the field and grain, three more dead men in two different saloons. The men in the saloons seemed to have been trying to drink themselves to death before the disease could get them. He also found eight more people in two other hotels.

On a sudden flash of insight he looked for a doctor's office. When he found it, he found six more dead people— four men, a woman, and a little boy.

Twenty-seven dead people so far. No wounds, same pallor. Definitely an epidemic so far. He decided not to run. There was no place to go, He was either infected or he wasn't. He decided to go through the doctor's things, see if he could find any notes. If the population had evacuated the town in the face of the disease, the doctor had probably taken his notes with him, but he might have left something behind.

First, though, Clint was hungry, and he had to take care of that.

In search of food, he spotted a café, went there, tied Eclipse off outside, entered a kitchen. It was fully stocked. He wanted something quick, so he made some bacon and eggs, soaked some leftover biscuits in the grease to soften them up. He found a shed out back with some vegetables and cured meats. If he was there long enough, he'd make himself a bigger meal. For the moment, bacon and eggs would do. And some good, strong coffee. He topped it off with a bottle of whiskey from a nearby small saloon that had no bodies in it. He grabbed a bottle of the most expensive whiskey, and this time drank half of it down.

So fortified, he took Eclipse to the livery, unsaddled him, brushed him, fed him, and left him there to rest.

Having taken care of his horse, Clint returned to the doctor's office to see what he could find out.

Not much, as it turned out.

He sat at the doctor's desk, went through some drawers. He found one note about a man who had come in with symptoms—weak, feverish, unable to keep food down. It was the last page in a notebook, and there was no new one around. The doctor must have taken it with him. According to the date in the book, the first man had come in to see him two months ago.

Two months for the disease to kill the town. Less, probably. He had no way of knowing when the people had actually left, although his best guess was less than a week ago. The beer was still cold.

Where had they gone?

How had they known they wouldn't be taking the disease with them?

And were they really gone?

He had no way of knowing how large the town really was. He'd searched the same general area, had come up with twenty-seven dead. What if they had moved to the other end of town, drawn a deadline in the street? Nobody allowed to cross from either side.

It was getting late. In the morning he'd saddle Eclipse and ride the length of the town, make sure it really was abandoned. There might still be some people who had remained behind.

He went back to the café, cooked himself a steak dinner with vegetables, washed it all down with coffee and the rest of that bottle of whiskey. He found a pallet in the back room, decided not to use any of the beds in the hotels. No point in taking unnecessary chances.

THREE

When he woke the next morning, he forgot for a moment where he was. There was a little light coming from a small window in the back. Then it hit him. He put his hands to his face, felt the skin, then looked at his hands. They were steady, the skin was smooth. He sat up on the pallet and took stock. He could breathe, he could see, and he felt all right. So far, so good.

He sat up, pulled on his boots, then stood up. He waited a moment, and when he didn't fall down, he left the back room, went into the kitchen. He took the time to make himself some steak and eggs. There was no hurry. If he was sick, he was sick. He could have ridden to the next town and found a doctor, but if he was infected, he'd be killing another group of people.

He wondered why nobody had posted a sign outside of town. A sign announcing QUARANTINE or something like it would have been helpful. It would have kept him from riding into this town.

He finished eating and cleaned up. Not that he needed to. Force of habit.

He walked to the livery, saddled Eclipse, and walked him

outside. That's when it occurred to him—he hadn't seen any dead horses.

Clint rode the length and width of the town. It was large enough to have been divided in two, but it hadn't been. No deadline. But he did find something.

He was checking out some of the buildings when he went into the kitchen of another small café. There was a frying pan on the stove, and the smell of cooked meat in the air. He went to the pan, stuck the tip of his finger in, pulled it back. There was grease in there, and it was still hot. He touched it to his tongue. Bacon.

There was somebody else alive in town.

He looked around, found lots of dirty plates. Recently used plates. Whoever it was didn't bother to clean up behind themselves the way he had.

He left the café, stopped just outside, scanned the streets, the buildings across the way. Where was this person sleeping? How large an area in town were they living in?

There was a saloon across the street. He crossed and went inside, went behind the bar. It was much the same as the other saloons he had been in—dirty glasses and empty bottles, but nothing recent.

Even at the café across the street. No whiskey, just glasses with remnants of water in them. No beer, no whiskey, unless the person had drunk them in another saloon.

Or they didn't drink.

Or it was a child.

A child who could cook?

A girl?

He went back outside.

Was he looking for a little girl?

He stepped into the middle of the street.

"Hello!" he shouted.

No answer.

"I know you're here," he said, louder. "I just want to help you."

Still no answer.

"I rode into town yesterday. I can see what happened here. Are you sick?"

He waited, but there was still no answer. Whoever it was could have been watching him from any window. Or they were already in another part of town.

He continued across the street to Eclipse.

"How you feeling, boy?" he asked, rubbing the horse's nose. "You're taking this very well. Actually, I'm taking it pretty well. I could be getting pretty sick in a little while, and maybe a doctor could help me. But if I go to find a doctor, I could make a lot of the people sick. So tell me, big boy, what do I do?"

Eclipse just stared at him. He had no answers. Maybe that was because the disease apparently did not affect animals. In addition to seeing no dead horses, Clint had not seen any dead dogs or cats, or livestock.

Well, one thing he could do was find the person who seemed to be the only survivor in town. Or else he could sit down and wait to die, but that was never his style.

"Where are you?" he called out, mounting up. "I just want to help you."

He rode Eclipse through town, yelling like he was the town crier.

In the end, he depended on Eclipse to entice her out. He went back to the café where he or she had eaten last, left the big gelding right outside. Eclipse attracted a lot of attention. He was hard to resist, especially for a child.

Clint found a place from where he could watch, and settled in to wait.

It didn't take long.

FOUR

As Clint watched, a little girl with blond hair came out of one of the buildings, looked around carefully, then started walking toward Eclipse. She was wearing a soiled yellow dress, her bare legs and arms also in need of a wash. Her hair was as yellow as the dress.

She walked carefully toward the horse, still looking around for Clint. He was sure that at first sight of him, she would break and run. He needed to sneak up on her once her attention was completely on Eclipse.

He knew the effect the big gelding had on people, especially children. He also knew that Eclipse would do nothing to harm the child. The Darley Arabian may not have liked being touched by strangers, but he'd never do anything to a child who tried to pet him.

The girl moved closer to the big horse. When she got around in front of him and extended her hand, the horse bent his head so she could reach him. She was now completely entranced by him, and it was time for Clint to make his move.

He came out the door of the hardware store and sneaked across the street to her side, then started moving slowly toward her.

Eclipse lowered his massive head enough for the child to rub his nose. As Clint got closer, he realized the girl was talking to the horse.

"You're a good boy, ain'tcha?" she said. "You're a good boy, and a big boy. How'd you get here? Where's the man who rode you?" She rubbed his nose harder. "Can you take me out of here? Can ya? I'll bet if I could get on your back, I could ride you away from here."

Clint was behind her now. He said, "I can help you ride him."

She whirled around, wide-eyed, stared at him, and then tried to run. He was too fast for her, and grabbed her.

"Let me go, let me go!" she shouted, trying to kick him.

"Take it easy," he told her. "Come on now. We have to help each other."

She continued to struggle.

"Don't you want to ride my horse?"

She struggled a bit more, than stopped and looked up at him. She had the bluest eyes he'd ever seen, a beautiful but grubby-looking little girl.

"He's—he's yours?"

"That's right."

"I can ride him?"

"Sure you can."

"Can you—can you take me away from here? I don't like it here."

"I don't much like it either," Clint said, "but I can't leave just yet. When I do, though, I'll take you with me. Where are your parents?"

"My mother and father . . . they left me here."

"Left you? But why?"

"I was sick, and they weren't. They said I was going to die and they had to leave."

"Who told them you were going to die?"

"The doctor."

"What's your name?"

"Emily."

"How long ago did they leave, Emily?"

"I—I ain't sure. Mister . . . are you gonna die? All the grown-ups, they either left, or died. There's lots of dead bodies in this town."

"I know," he said. "I found them. Look, Emily, we have to help each other. If I let you go, do you promise not to run?"

She thought about it a moment, then said, "Okay, I promise."

He released her. She immediately turned, but instead of running, she reached for Eclipse's nose again.

"What's his name?" she asked.

They went into the café where he'd discovered the hot frying pan with the bacon grease.

"Will Eclipse be all right alone out there?" she asked.

"He'll be fine."

"Will he get sick?"

"I don't think so," Clint said. "I haven't seen any dead animals around here."

He walked her to a table and they sat down.

"Emily, have you been taking care of yourself all this time? Since your parents left?"

"Yes," she said. "When they left, I was in my bed. I think I slept for a very long time. When I woke up, I felt weak and thirsty. I—I got up, and got dressed and went looking for Momma and Papa, but I couldn't find them. I couldn't find anybody, except for dead people. So I made myself something to eat."

"And you've been doing that ever since?"

She nodded. "Mama showed me how to cook so I could help around the house."

"How old are you?"

"Ten."

"Can you show me where you lived?" Clint asked.

"Maybe I can find something there that will tell me how long your parents have been gone. Or where they've gone."

"I can show you."

"Is it far?"

"Not far," she said, "if we ride."

He smiled at her and said, "Let's ride."

FIVE

Clint put Emily in the saddle and walked alongside her so he could catch her if she fell off. She directed him this way and that until they came to a stop in front of a small, one-floor, wood-framed house.

"We lived in there," she said, pointing.

"Okay," he said, lifting her off Eclipse's back to the ground, "show me."

They walked to the front door, where she balked.

"Emily? Are there any . . . dead people in there?" he asked.

"N-No."

"Then we can go in, right?"

"Y-Yes."

"Are you afraid?"

"No," she said, "I'm sad."

She reached for his hand, grabbed it, and they went into the house together.

"Okay," he said, "why don't you sit on the sofa while I look around?"

"No," she said, squeezing his hand, "I want to stay with you."

"All right," he said, "show me your parents' room."

"This way . . ."

She took him down a hall to a bedroom which obviously belonged to adults. However, it also looked as if it had been hit by a cyclone.

"I didn't do it," she said.

"Do what?"

"Make this mess," she said. "I didn't do it."

"Oh, honey, I know you didn't do this. Your parents obviously packed in a hurry."

"Because they were afraid I'd make them sick?" she asked.

"Not you," he said. "The disease."

"But . . . what disease? Why didn't I die?"

"Obviously," he said, "you were immune to the disease."

"Huh? What's im-immune?"

"It means that while the disease killed a lot of other people, it didn't kill you."

"Is that why my momma and papa didn't get sick? Because they was immune?"

"I think so. I think a lot of people were immune, and they decided to leave town."

What they hadn't done was try to warn travelers about the disease that had ravaged their town, or burn the town down, which was what they should have done. But if they had, they would also have burned up Emily.

"What's your last name, Emily?"

"Patterson," she said. "My name is Emily Rose Patterson."

"Well, Emily Rose Patterson, let's take a quick look around and see if your parents left anything that will tell me where they are. And then we'll go and get something to eat. How's that sound?"

"Good, I guess."

"And you know what?" he said. "I'm a terrible cook. Maybe you could cook something for us to eat?"

She brightened at that.

"We could go to Flo's Café," she said. "I ain't cooked for myself there yet. There's bound to be a lot of food."

"Good," Clint said. "After we look around, we'll ride Eclipse over to the café."

"Okay!"

Still holding hands, they looked around the room, and then walked through the rest of the house. Clint found nothing that would tell him where the parents had gone. He also did not find any mail that would tell him where some of their relatives might live.

They left the house. He put Emily back in the saddle, then mounted behind her. After that, she directed him to Flo's Café.

SIX

Emily knew her way around town very well. She easily guided Clint to Flo's Café. They went inside to the kitchen, and once he saw how at home she was there and that she didn't need any help, he went and sat at a table.

Obviously there were many citizens of Medicine Bow who had not succumbed to the disease and had left town. This was a good sign for him. It was possible that he'd be one of those people who was immune, but it would take a while before he'd be comfortable that he had survived.

He also wondered if, after a reasonable amount of time went by, the citizens would come back, or if they had given up on the town and started over somewhere else. If they came back, perhaps Emily's parents would come back with them. However, if they had started over somewhere else . . . well, there was no guarantee that the whole town had stayed together. Maybe they would have split up, rather than be reminded of the disease every time they looked at one another.

Soon the smells from the kitchen wafted out to him. If those aromas were any indication, Emily really did know how to cook.

When she came out, she was carrying two plates teeming and steaming with eggs and vegetables.

"The meat is bad," she told him. "But there were plenty of eggs and vegetables left behind."

He frowned. The steaks he'd prepared for himself had tasted kind of funny, but he'd assumed that was a result of his own cooking skills. Was it possible he'd eaten bad meat? If the disease didn't take him, would the bad meat kill him?

She sat across from him and said, "Go ahead, eat your food."

"Yes, ma'am."

"You didn't tell me your name," she said, as if scolding him. "My daddy always says people should introduce themselves."

"I'm sorry," he said. "My name is Clint Adams."

"Mr. Adams, what's your horse's name?"

"Well, you can call me Clint, Emily," he said. "And the horse's name is Eclipse."

"Eclipse," she said, was if tasting the word. She nodded. "I like that."

"I'm glad. By the way, these are the best eggs I've ever tasted." It was true, they were the best eggs he'd ever had . . . without meat.

"Thank you. I know my daddy likes his eggs with ham or bacon, and sometimes steak, but I just ate the last of the good bacon. Sorry. Like I said, the rest of the meat's no good anymore." She wrinkled her nose.

"Oh," she said suddenly, "I forgot the coffee."

Coffee? He hadn't smelled coffee. She left the table and hurried into the kitchen, then came out walking very carefully with a mug of coffee.

"Thank you," he said, accepting the mug. She ran back to the kitchen and returned with a glass of water for herself. She sat back down to eat. Clint wasn't sure about the water, which was why he'd been drinking beer or whiskey. He sipped the coffee. It was hot, but weak, although that didn't really matter.

"It's very good," he lied, putting the cup down. "You really are good in the kitchen, aren't you?"

"My momma says I am."

The child obviously loved her mother and father. How, he wondered, could they have left her behind without knowing for sure that the disease had taken her?

"Clint?"

"Yes?"

"How come you and me ain't dead?"

"Well," he said, "I guess we're just able to resist the disease, Emily. But from what you told me, you did get sick, right?"

"Oh, yes."

"But you didn't die," he said. "So I suppose I might still get sick . . ."

"And die?"

"Maybe," he said. "I hope not."

"Can't we leave before you get sick?"

"No, honey," he said. "First we have to make sure I don't have the disease. We don't want to take it with us to another town, do we?"

"I suppose not," she said, leaning her elbow on the table with her face in her hand. "But when can we leave?"

"Soon," he said. "I'm still feeling pretty good, so we may be able to leave soon."

She brightened. "We have the whole town to ourselves"—and then her expression soured—"but it kind of smells bad."

"All those dead people should have been buried," Clint told her. "The people must have been in a real hurry when they left here."

"I was in bed," she said, "but I could hear people shouting outside . . . and then it got quiet."

Clint figured if the townspeople left en masse, he should

be able to pick up some kind of trail once they got outside of town, depending on how long ago they left.

"What should we do after we eat?" she asked.

"I think we'll look around town some more," Clint said, "see if we can find some supplies that we'll need for our ride."

"Clint?"

"Yes."

"I'm glad I'm not alone anymore."

"So am I, Emily," he said. "So am I."

SEVEN

Before looking for supplies, Clint decided to go to city hall and see if he could find any notes that might indicate where the people had gone. Also the telegraph office.

City hall was first. Thankfully, they did not come across any more dead bodies.

"I ain't never been in city hall before," Emily said, her eyes wide.

"Why not?" Clint asked.

"Well . . . that's where the mayor works." She said it in hushed tones.

"Emily, can you tell me if the mayor got sick?"

"I don't know," she said.

"Okay. We're going to go to his office."

Her eyes widened even more. "The mayor's office?"

"That's right."

He took her hand and they entered the building. The mayor's office was on the second floor, in the back, rather than in the front, where he'd have a window overlooking the street.

When they got inside, Clint saw that it was a very large office. It had to be, to fit the large teakwood desk.

"Oh my," Emily said, looking around.

"Emily, you have a seat while I look around."

"All right."

She got up into one of the wooden chairs that faced the mayor's desk. Clint got behind the desk and sat down. There were some papers strewn across the top of it. He went through them, but there was nothing to tell him where the townspeople had gone. He started going through the drawers and Emily covered her mouth with her hands.

"What?" he asked.

"You're going through the mayor's drawers," she whispered.

"Well," he said, "the mayor's not here, so I think we're all right."

"Okay," she whispered.

He continued to go through the drawers, scanning papers, but there was nothing helpful.

"Okay," he said, sitting back. "I think we're finished here."

"What do we do now?"

"We're going to the telegraph office."

"Oh, good," she said. "I like that place." She got down from the chair. "I like the clackety-clack that the key makes."

"The key?"

"The telegraph key," she told him. "Didn't you know it was called that?"

"Well, yes, I did know that," he said. "Come on. Let's go."

He took her hand and they left the office, and the building.

"Which way is the telegraph office, Emily?" he asked.

"That way," she said, pointing. "A few blocks. Can I ride Eclipse?"

"Of course."

He lifted her up into the saddle and then they walked to the telegraph office.

"Do you want to come inside?" he asked.

"Yes," she said. "Clackety-clack."

"Clackety-clack," he repeated, and lifted her down.

They walked inside the office, which looked as if it had

been ransacked. There were yellow pieces of paper all over the floor, and desk.

"I don't hear the key," she complained.

"No, neither do I."

He walked around behind the desk to examine the key. It was quiet, but that didn't mean it wasn't working. He didn't know how to use to, though. He touched it, depressed it a few times, just eliciting a short clackety-clack for Emily, but he didn't know if anyone at the other end had heard it.

"Can you make it work?"

"No," he said. "I don't know how."

"Oh." She was obviously disappointed. Then she brightened. "Can I do it?"

She climbed on a chair and began to play with the key, making it go clackety-clackety-clackety. Clint wondered if anyone out there would hear it and send someone to investigate. Or if the key operator had sent any messages concerning the disease. Or had he died before he could?

He looked around at the yellow slips, but there were no telegrams that would help him.

He watched as Emily happily played with the key. He took a seat, decided to let her play with it to her heart's content, until she grew tired, while he tried to figure out their next move.

She spent a good half hour playing with the key. He sat in the chair with his chin in his hand, drifting off, until suddenly the chatter of the key stopped. When he opened his eyes, he saw her sitting there, staring at him, looking terrified.

"Hey, honey, what is it? What's wrong?"

"I—I thought you was dead, Clint."

"No, sweetie, no," he said, "I was just resting. Come here."

She came to him and he hugged her tightly, her little arms wrapped around his neck.

EIGHT

As they left the telegraph office, Clint asked, "Emily, have you been sleeping in your own bed?"

"No," she said, "it's too sad and scary. The house is so empty."

"Then where have you been sleeping?"

She shrugged. "A different place every night—but not where there's any dead people."

"Well," he said, "I can't blame you for that. I wouldn't want to sleep where there's dead people. So where do you think we should sleep tonight?"

"There's lots of bed I ain't slept in yet," she said. "Let's go and look!"

"Okay," he said, "let's go."

They walked around town—with Clint actually walking and Emily astride Eclipse—stopping in a building whenever she pointed it out. He was happy to let her do the choosing, thus keeping her mind busy.

They stopped in front of a small building and she said, "This was Aunt Kathy's boardinghouse."

"She was your aunt?" he asked.

"No, silly," she said. "That was the name of her board-inghouse."

"I see. Well, let's have a look."

He lifted her down from the horse and they went up the front steps to the porch. He tried the door and found it locked. Many of the buildings they'd check had been unlocked. Apparently, "Aunt Kathy" had thought to lock her door behind her. Maybe she was planning on coming back.

"I guess I'll have to force the door," he said. "Stand back."

Emily moved away. As Clint prepared to put his shoulder to the door, there was a shot. A bullet shattered the glass of the door and just missed his head. He leaped to the side, his hand on his gun.

He looked at Emily and said, "I guess there's somebody else alive in town."

"Are you all right?" she asked.

"I'm fine. Let's see if we can find out who this is. You stay there—and crouch down low."

"All right."

Clint took his gun out, reached over, and tapped on the door with the barrel.

"Hello inside the house? We don't mean you any harm. I've got little Emily Patterson out here. Apparently she was immune to the disease that killed so many people."

He listened, but there was no reply.

"My name is Clint Adams. I only rode into town yester-day. Are you all right?"

There was no answer, then a woman's voice said, "Go away! I have a rifle."

"I know that," he called back. "Your bullet just missed me. But why are you shooting?"

"You're not stealing anything from me," she shouted back.

"What makes you think I want to steal?"

No answer.

"Look, are you . . . Aunt Kathy? I have a little girl out here with me."

"Prove it!"

"Emily, call out to the lady."

"What do I say?" she whispered.

"Just say hello, and tell her your name."

"Hello," the child called out. "This is Emily."

There was a long moment of silence and then the woman said, "Emily? Is that you?"

"It's me," Emily said.

There was the sound of a lock turning, and then the door opened slowly. A woman stuck her head out and her eyes went right to Emily.

"It is you."

"Hello, Aunt Kathy."

"Come here, child," the woman said. She put her rifle down as Emily rushed into her arms. The woman hugged her tightly, crying. Emily turned her head and directed a puzzled look Clint's way. He holstered his gun.

"I'm so glad you're alive," the woman said.

"I'm glad you're alive, too," the child said.

The woman held her at arm's length and asked, "What happened to your parents?"

"They left me."

"What? They left you behind?"

"I was sick," Emily said. "I think they thought I was going to die."

"But still," the woman said, "how could they leave you?"

Finally, she looked over at Clint.

"Mr. Adams?"

"That's right."

"Please," she said, "come inside."

"Thank you," he said. "You're not going to shoot at me again, are you?"

"No," she said, "I promise I won't."

They went into the house, closing the door behind them. The woman set the rifle aside and turned to face Clint.

"I'm sorry about the rifle," she said. "When people started dying, there were looters. I had to fight to keep them out of here."

"Did you get sick at all?" he asked.

"I did," she said. "I succumbed just before the mass exodus began. I was in bed when they all left."

"So was Emily."

The woman put her hand on the girl's head.

"Poor dear," she said. "How could her parents leave without knowing for sure if she was alive or dead?"

"I suppose they panicked."

"I guess you're right. Have the two of you eaten?"

"We have," Clint said. "Emily cooked for me over at Flo's Café. We were actually looking for someplace to spend the night."

"Well, stop looking," she said. "I have plenty of empty beds here."

"How does that sound, Emily?" Clint asked.

"It sounds good to me!"

Clint looked at the woman. She was in her thirties, very attractive despite looking somewhat bedraggled.

"Do I keep calling you Aunt Kathy?"

"My name is Kathleen Logan," she said. " 'Aunt Kathy's' just the name of the boardinghouse, Mr. Adams."

"My name is Clint," he said, "Kathleen."

"How about some pie?" she asked Emily.

"Apple?"

"Of course."

"Yay!"

"And you, Clint?"

"With coffee?" he asked.

"Of course."

"Yay!" he said with a grin at Emily.

NINE

They went into the kitchen and Kathy served them their pie with coffee for Clint and hot tea for Emily.

"I'm sorry, but the milk went bad a long time ago," she said.

"That's something Emily hasn't been able to tell me, Kathy," he said. "When did all of this happen?"

"Oh, it started about six weeks ago. Within two weeks, many people were dead."

"Were they burying any of the dead?"

"Yes," she said, "there's a graveyard just outside of town. But soon the people decided to just pull out. They stopped burying people and started packing to leave about three weeks ago. I—I got sick and ended up in bed. I was unconscious when the last of them finally pulled out, probably about a week ago."

"Everyone?"

"I don't know," she said. "As I said, I was unconscious in bed."

"But when you woke up, they were all gone?"

"Far as I can tell," she said. "That was about a week ago."

"And you have enough food to just hole up here?"

"Remember," she said, "I was running a boardinghouse.

I had enough food to feed my guests. Once it was just me, I had plenty."

"Well, poor Emily has been scrounging all around town," Clint said.

"I'm sorry she didn't come here sooner," Kathy said. "I would have taken her in."

Emily was eating her pie and not really listening to them.

"Did anyone die in this house?"

"One man early on. We were able to bury him. The rest of my boarders got scared and left. So there were no bodies in my house when I woke up—thank God."

"Why didn't you leave when you were able to, Kathy?" he asked.

"I thought about it," she said. "But this place is all I have. I—I couldn't just leave it. Besides, maybe the people will come back."

"I doubt it," Clint said. "In fact, I'm surprised the town isn't overrun with scavengers now, the smell of death is so pervasive with all the unburied bodies."

"Scavengers?" she asked. "You mean . . . looters?"

"I'm talking about the four-legged kind," he said, "not to mention buzzards. I assume it's because most of the bodies are inside."

"But . . . what if they do come? Would they try to get inside?"

"Once they got hungry enough, and brave enough," Clint said, "probably."

"I have noticed the terrible smell," she said, wrinkling her nose.

"Bodies lying around for weeks," Clint said. "I'm surprised the scavengers haven't been here yet. Are there any other people left in town besides you and Emily?"

"Not that I know of," she said. "You think that Emily and I being here has kept the animals out? That they wouldn't come in while there was somebody in town still alive?"

"I don't think so," Clint said. "Emily is a small child, and you've been inside most of the time, right? Haven't been around town much?"

"Yes, that's right."

"Then I don't think your presence alone would keep them away," he said. "Maybe there are more people around. That would probably do it." He looked across the table at Emily, who was licking her plate clean.

"Would you like another slice of pie, Emily?" Kathy asked her.

"Oh, yes, please."

While she cut another slice, Clint said, "Emily, have you seen any other people in town the past few weeks?"

"Do you mean the men?"

"What men?" he asked.

Kathy placed the second slice of pie in front of her and looked at Clint. He shook his head, and she sat back down at the table.

"The men I hide from."

"How many men, Emily?"

She shrugged. "I don't know. Three or four. When I see them, I hide."

Clint wondered what three or four men were still doing around town. It certainly wasn't burying bodies. Perhaps, as Kathy had said, they were looters.

"Maybe," he said, "I should have another look around town."

"You can leave Emily with me," she said.

"That's good," he said. "Is there a livery stable near here?"

"A couple of blocks."

"That'll have to do," he said. "I'll want to bed my horse down properly."

"Take your time," she said. "I'll enjoy Emily's company. And yours, when it comes to it."

"I'll take care of my horse tonight," Clint said, "and do another search around town tomorrow."

"What makes you think you might see them tomorrow when you haven't seen them up to now?" she asked.

"Up to now," he told her, "I haven't been looking for them."

TEN

Clint walked Eclipse to the livery stable. It was clean, with no bodies around. He unsaddled him, brushed and fed him, then bedded him down for the night.

Clint was about to leave the stable when he noticed some tracks in the dirt. He crouched down to examine them. They'd been made by a man's boots, and they looked fresh—not that day, but pretty fresh.

He followed them out the front door, where they mixed with his tracks. He decided not to follow them any farther tonight. In the morning, this was where he'd start.

He walked back to the boardinghouse, let himself in the unlocked front door, and then locked it. He found them still in the kitchen.

"Is she still eating pie?" he asked.

"No," Kathy said, "we're just talking."

"Well, maybe Emily should be getting to bed," Clint suggested.

"I think," Kathy said, "she needs a bath first."

"What?" Emily asked.

"That sounds like a good idea to me," Clint said.

"It wouldn't hurt you to take one, too," Kathy added.

"Yeah," Emily said, "if I have to take a bath, so do you, Clint."

"Sure, little girl," Clint said. "I'll take mine right after you take yours and get into bed."

"Come on," Kathy said to Emily, "I'll help you." She looked at Clint. "I'll draw you one later."

"Okay."

"Have some coffee while you wait."

"Suits me," Clint said.

After she left the kitchen with Emily, Clint poured himself a cup of coffee, took a look out the back window while he drank it. He could see other houses. He wondered if there were people hiding in any of them, the way Kathy was staying in her house. He'd have to check them out the next day.

He got impatient waiting for Kathy to come back, so he cut himself another slice of pie.

He was finishing yet another cup of coffee when she came back into the kitchen.

"Is she down?"

"She went out right away," Kathy said, sitting across from him.

"You look like you're ready to turn in," he commented. "It's still early."

"Time hasn't meant much for a while," she told him. "I sleep when I'm tired, which is most of the time. By the way, I drew your bath. If you want it while it's hot, you better go now."

"You going to be okay?" he asked.

"I'll be fine," she said. "I'll clean up in here."

"I shouldn't be long."

"I laid out some clean clothes for you."

"Husband's?"

"Some of my tenants left clothes behind when they ran," she said. "I guessed at the size."

"I'll let you know if they fit."

"Just go down the hall," she said. "I'll empty it when you're done."

He walked down the hall, found the room with the tub. She had folded the clothes and set them on a chair. He stripped down and got into the tub. He sat back and just let the hot water soak in for a while, then picked up the soap and cloth and washed off all the dirt. He had just finished washing his hair when the door opened and Kathy stepped in.

"Oh," he said, "I'm almost finished."

"That's okay," she said. "I just thought I'd check and make sure the water was still hot."

"It's okay," he said, staring at her.

"No," she said, "I better check."

She walked over to the tub, leaned over, and put her hand in. That close he could smell her.

"You know," she said, swirling the soapy water, "I've been lonely for a while. I've been missing . . . things."

"What things?"

"Companionship," she said, "somebody to talk to, maybe somebody to take care of."

"I don't need taking care of," he said. "But I'm sure Emily does."

"Well," she said, "I didn't mean that kind of taking care of."

"What kind did you mean?"

She knelt by the tub. The cotton dress she was wearing stuck to her because of the steam in the room from the hot water. He could see her firm breasts, and the outlines of her hard nipples.

"This kind," she said. She reached into the water, found his cock, and grasped it. It had already begun to get hard, so it swelled even more in her hand. She began to stroke it up and down.

"Oh," he said, "that kind."

ELEVEN

He sat back in the tub while she stroked him with her right hand. With her left hand, she unbuttoned her dress until one breast almost fell out. It was lovely, pale, and round with a hard pink nipple. He reached out with his left hand to cup it, fondle it, weigh it, swipe the nipple with his thumb. She gasped, released him, stood up, and let the dress fall to the floor. Then she stepped into the tub with him. Sat down across from him, with her legs inside his. She pulled her knees up and scooted closer to him so she could reach for him and take him in both hands this time. She stroked his shaft with her right hand, cupped his balls with her left. He leaned forward to kiss her, and her mouth opened beneath his eagerly. He slid his hands around her and pulled her closer to him. She put her legs outside his, and wrapped them around his waist as he pulled her into his lap. Suddenly, just like that, he was inside her, and she gasped.

"Oh, God," she said, biting him on the shoulder as she started to move up and down on him.

He grunted as she came down on him, her nails raking his back.

"Shhh, shhh," she said in his ear, even though he wasn't making much noise. "We don't want to wake Emily."

"Then we have to stay here," he said. "We can't move to the bedroom."

She tightened her legs around him, and her insides seemed to grip him tighter.

"Here's just fine with me," she said into his ear, then bit his earlobe. She kissed his neck and shoulders as she bounced up and down on him, splashing water onto the floor. She let her head fall back and bit her lips as she moved faster. He placed his hands against the small of her back, supporting her. She grew flushed, and her breathing became labored as she neared her time. Suddenly, she was a frenzy of movement on him and it was all he could do to keep her from leaping out of the tub. And through it all she managed to keep quiet, even when a small trail of blood made its way down her chin from where she had bitten her lip. He held her tightly by the hips until he erupted inside her, biting back his own grunts. The water splashed and splashed and then suddenly they both stopped and slumped against each other in the tub.

"Oh God," she said with her mouth against his neck, "I needed that."

"I know," he said. "It's good to be alive."

"Exactly!" she said.

They sat that way until the water started to cool, and then she drew back first.

"I'm not . . ." she said.

"I know," he said.

Suddenly embarrassed, she got out of the tub and picked up her dress. She turned, looked at him, holding her dress in front of her, then went to the door, peered out, and left.

Clint got out of the tub, dried himself off, and tried on the clothes Kathy had left for him. They fit pretty well, although they probably had belonged to a heavier man.

He carried his gun belt down the hall to the living room, where Kathy was sitting, wearing a different dress.

"You can have your pick of any room upstairs," she said. "I put Emily in the front room. It's next to mine and I'll be able to hear her."

"Well," he said, "maybe I'll take a room in the back, then."

"Do you really need to keep that gun with you in the house?" she asked.

"This gun has become a part of me," he said. "And I'm not convinced there aren't other people here. I saw some tracks at the livery."

"What kind of tracks? Animals?"

"A man."

"One man?"

"So far," Clint said.

"What are you going to do?"

"I'll follow the tracks tomorrow morning," he said. "I want to find out if we're alone or not."

"What if we aren't?"

"Then I'll find out who the others are, and what they want."

"And if there aren't any others?"

"I'll have to decide what to do then," Clint said. "I plan on leaving town, but I don't know when. I have to make sure I'm not sick."

"How do you feel now?" she asked.

"I feel pretty good," he said, "especially after my bath." She blushed.

"How long did it take you to fall sick?" he asked.

"A lot of people had died before I started to feel sick," she said, "and then . . . I don't know, I was probably in bed after a couple of days."

"Well," he said, "tomorrow will be two days for me. If I'm not sick after, say, five, I guess it will be safe for me to leave."

"Where will you go?"

"I was thinking I'd take Emily and try to find her parents," Clint said, "but that was when I thought we were here alone."

"You want to leave her with me?"

"Do you intend to stay here?"

"I—I can't just leave my house," she said.

"What happens when you run out of food?"

"I'm sure there must still be food in town," she said.

"Sure," he said, "canned goods. I think there are still some on the shelves of the general store, and certainly in some of the other homes. We can go around and collect as much as we can so you can stock up, but it's got to run out eventually."

"I guess I'll deal with that situation when it comes," she said.

"The other thing is all the dead bodies," he said. "If you're going to stay, I can't just leave them where they are."

"B-But how can you dig so many graves?"

"Not so many," he said. "One mass grave. Then I'll use a buckboard to take the bodies to the hole."

"You would do that?"

"Why not?" Clint asked. "I have to be here for another few days anyway. I can probably do it over that time."

"I'll help," she said. "I mean, since you're doing it for me."

"Okay," he said, "maybe you can drive the buckboard."

"No" she said, "I'll help you dig."

"Sure," he said, "but first I'll find out if there's anyone else in town. If there is, then I might have help burying the dead."

"All right, then," she said. "I guess I better turn in. It looks like we'll have some busy days ahead of us." She stood up. "I can't tell you how much I appreciate that you're here, Clint."

She blushed again when she realized how that sounded, and quickly went up the steps to her room.

TWELVE

Clint woke up the next morning and spent a few moments taking stock of himself. He felt fine, especially after a good night's sleep. He sat up, put his feet on the ground, flexed his hands, stretched his arms over his head, rubbed his hands over his face. Then stood up.

There was no sign of weakness, or illness.

He grabbed the fresh clothes Kathy had supplied and put them on, then strapped on his gun and went downstairs. Halfway down he could hear Emily's voice, and smell the bacon.

As he entered the kitchen, he saw Kathy and Emily at the stove, laughing and cooking.

"What are you two up to?" he asked.

"Clint!" Emily shouted. "We're makin' breakfast—a real breakfast, with bacon!"

"That sounds great."

"You go and sit in the dining room," Kathy said. "I'll bring out some coffee and biscuits."

"Okay."

He went out to the large table where Kathy would normally feed her boarders. In moments, Kathy was there with the promised coffee and biscuits. She also brought some butter.

"Bacon and eggs will be right out," she said.

"I'll be here."

She smiled and returned to the kitchen.

Clint buttered a biscuit and bit into it. It was light and fluffy, wonderful. He washed it down with coffee, which was very good. It could have been stronger, but it was better than the coffee Emily had made for him.

Kathy and Emily came out with plates and platters and set them on the table, then sat down. The table was very long, but they sat at the same end with Clint.

"Go ahead," Kathy said, spooning eggs onto Emily's plate, "help yourself."

"You didn't have to do this," he said, glad that she had.

"I wanted to," she said. "It's been a while since I've cooked for people."

Clint filled his plate with bacon and eggs, took more biscuits, and poured himself some more coffee. After that, they all just started eating.

"This is so good," Emily said. "This is better than my cooking."

"Thank you," Kathy said.

"Is her coffee better than mine, Clint?"

"Well," he said, "it's different."

"That's okay," she said, "I know I don't make good coffee. But Kathy's gonna teach me to cook better."

"She is? That's great."

"Yeah, it is!"

They went back to eating and before long all the platters were empty.

"Emily and I will clean up," Kathy said.

"I'll help."

"No," she said, "that's okay. You finish the coffee."

He decided not to argue. As they carried everything back to the kitchen, he poured himself the last of the coffee. By the time Kathy came back out, he was finished.

"Emily is such a good girl," she said. "She doesn't complain, even though I know she misses her parents."

"I know," Clint said. "She's . . . good." He stood up.

"Are you going out now?"

"Yes."

"To look for those people?"

"To look for any people," he said, "but I'll start with those tracks I found at the livery."

"Do you want me to come with you?"

"No," he said, "you have to stay here with Emily. I'll be back later."

"For lunch?" she asked. "I can make lunch."

"That'd be great," Clint told her, because it would give her something to do. "I'll be back for lunch."

She nodded. He went to the front door and out. As he was walking to the street, the front door opened and Emily ran out, almost screaming.

"Clint! Clint!"

He turned. She ran to him and wrapped her arms around his waist.

"Are you coming back?" she asked.

He removed her arms, then crouched down in front of her and held her by the shoulders.

"Emily, yes, of course I'm coming back," he told her. "I'm just going to have another look around town to see if I can find anybody else."

"You wouldn't leave me, would you?"

"No, honey," he said, hugging her to him, "I wouldn't leave you." She'd already been left by too many people.

He walked her back to the front porch, where Kathy was waiting. She put her arms around the girl and they both watched as Clint walked away.

Clint walked to the livery, where he could pick up the tracks he had seen. But first he checked on Eclipse, to make sure the gelding was okay.

"How you doing, buddy?" Clint asked. He ran his hand over the horse's flanks. He thought about taking the horse, but decided to go on foot. He wasn't really worried about somebody coming to the stable and stealing him. Eclipse wouldn't permit that. One or two men would have a hard time taking the Darley Arabian anywhere he didn't want to go.

"I'll be back later," he said, and left the livery.

The man's boot tracks were easy to pick up and follow. They led Clint to a part of town he really hadn't spent much time in yet. The town had some stockyards, which were, of course, empty at the moment. The lack of dead cows or horses further enforced his assumption that animals had not been affected by the disease.

The tracks seemed to lead to a stable behind the stockyards. He approached carefully, just in case Kathy was right and he was about to run into a bunch of looters.

Inside the stable he didn't find looters, but he did find loot—and a lot of it. It was stacked in crates and cartons in the center of the stable. He wondered who had done the stacking, how many of them, and how they intended to transport the stuff.

He walked around the pile of loot, checking the ground. There were several tracks in the dirt, all looking like men's boots. It could have been three men who never left town and stayed behind to clean it out, or three men who rode in, found it abandoned, and figured they could clean up. Either way, they wouldn't be happy to see him. Clint wasn't sure how the law would stand on this, and they probably weren't either. It might depend on whether or not the law considered Medicine Bow to be a ghost town. If it was, then the contents were probably all fair game.

His intention had been to scour the town for other people. And, in fact, there might still be others in town like Kathy, who had fallen ill, but recovered and stayed behind to protect what was theirs. And maybe they were also doing what Kathy did and staying indoors. They were no danger to anyone. The three looters, however, might act violently if they saw someone else in town. He needed to find them, disarm them, and then question them. And rather than going out to locate them, the smart thing might be to just stay right where he was and let them come to him. Sooner or later, they'd be coming back with some more loot.

Clint wondered where they had put their own horses. While he'd seen the tracks of one man at the livery, there were no horses and no tracks left by horses.

THIRTEEN

By lunchtime nobody had returned. They could have been in any part of town, loading up the buckboard that had left the tracks he later found behind the building. Kathy and Emily would be worried about him, and he could always return later to find the looters.

He thought about wiping out his tracks, but the marks he'd leave behind would probably be even more obvious than his footprints. He doubted the looters would come back and notice his tracks in the dirt. He'd come back later, see if they had returned.

Walking back to Kathy's boardinghouse, he wondered how he had missed seeing fresh buckboard tracks around town. Or any sign of the three men. Was it possible they were looting a part of town he simply had not been in yet?

When he got back to the house, he checked the ground in front to see if anyone had been there since he'd left. As long as he was staying with Kathy, they'd have to take some precautions against the looters until he found them.

As he entered the house, he could once again smell what the girls were cooking. It looked like Kathy was serious about using some of the food she'd stocked up since all her boarders left. If she wasn't careful, she'd leave herself short when he and Emily left.

Unless he decided to leave Emily behind. He had told the little girl he wouldn't leave her, but wouldn't she be better off with a woman than with him? And a woman like Kathy, who was used to taking care of people?

Or maybe he could convince Kathy to leave with them, and he could leave both of them in the next town.

"I'm back," he called out.

There was no answer.

"Emily? Kathy?"

Suddenly, the two girls appeared in the doorway of the kitchen, but there was a man behind them, holding a gun. They both looked too frightened to talk.

The man was taller than Kathy, tall enough to look at Clint over her head.

"Just take it easy and nobody will get hurt," the man said.

Clint didn't believe him. He knew a man bent on killing when he saw one. But Clint wouldn't kill him until he found out if he was alone.

"What do you want?"

"H-He came in the back door," Kathy said. "He said he wanted—"

"Shut up!"

"He hurt Kathy, Clint!" Emily yelled.

"Shut up, both of you!" the man shouted. Both girls flinched.

"What do you want?"

"The big one here tells me your name is Jones," the man said. "Well, okay, Jones—Clint Jones?"

"Yeah, that's right."

"Put your gun on the floor."

"Not just yet."

The man had the gun pointed at Clint from between the two girls. Now he cocked the hammer back.

"Do like I tell you."

"Are you one of three, or are there more of you?" Clint asked.

"Three?"

"Yeah, I saw the tracks of three of you, over in the stock-yards where you've got your loot. Just the three of you?"

"First," the man said, "you tell me how many of you there are."

"Just me," Clint said.

"Why are you here?"

"I was passing through, didn't know about the disease," Clint said.

"Did you get sick?" the man asked.

"Not yet. You?"

"No," the man said, "we knew we were immune. That's why we came back."

Well, that made sense. They left with everyone else, but came back to loot the town.

"Then you know where everyone else went?"

"Sure."

"Where?"

"Why do you wanna know that?"

"I want to take this little girl to her parents."

"Her parents?" the man asked. "The ones who left her here to die? Why?"

"Because they're her parents."

"Never mind." He waggled the barrel of the gun. "Let's get back to your gun. Drop it."

"I told you," Clint said, "I can't."

"I'll kill one of these bitches."

"To do that, you'd have to take the gun off me and point it at one of them," Clint told him. "When you do that, I'll kill you."

The man laughed.

"You think you're that fast?"

"Lots of people think so," Clint said. "See, my last name is not really Jones."

"I didn't think so. What is it?"

"Adams."

The man froze.

"Clint Adams?"

"That's right."

He saw by the look in the man's eyes that he was going to pull the trigger. Clint drew. He had only the sliver of space between Kathy and Emily to work with. His bullet went right between them and hit the man in the belly. He grunted, staggered back, and dropped his gun.

"Move!" Clint shouted at the girls.

They did. Kathy went right, and Emily went left. Clint moved into the kitchen to check the body. The man was dead.

"Are you two all right?" he asked, coming back into the dining room.

Emily ran to Clint and wrapped her arms around his waist. Kathy said, "Yeah, we're fine."

"How long has he been here?" he asked.

"About half an hour," she said. "He just came in the back door and surprised us."

"Did he say how many more there were?"

"No," she said, "but didn't you say there were three?"

"That's all I saw the tracks for." He ejected the spent shell from his gun, slid in a live one, and holstered it.

"He did say that there was nobody else in town," she told him. "Just me and Emily."

"How did he know about me?"

"I—" She turned her head. He remembered what Emily had said about the man hurting her.

"He hurt her, Clint," Emily said, "and he said he would hurt me if she didn't answer his questions."

"Okay," he said. "I get it." He went to the back door and looked out.

"I didn't see anybody in front," he said, "so I guess he was here alone."

"But how did he know about me?"

"He must have been checking the houses around here," Clint said. "I think they've been looting a certain section of town. They were probably planning on coming here next."

"What will happen when this man doesn't get back to them?" Kathy asked.

"They'll come looking for him."

"Two of them?"

"Let's hope it's only two," he said. "Wait." He went back into the kitchen and checked the bottom of the dead man's boots. "Damn it!"

"What?"

"He isn't one of the three," Clint said.

"So there's three out there?"

"Three," Clint said to her, "or more."

FOURTEEN

Clint dragged the body out of the kitchen and all the way to the nearest house. He checked it first to make sure it was empty, then dragged the body inside and put it where it couldn't be seen from a window.

When he came back, Kathy had finished cleaning the blood from the kitchen floor.

"Where's Emily?"

"She's upstairs." She tossed aside the rag she'd used to clean the floor. "What did you do with . . . him?"

"I gave him to your next-door neighbor."

"What?"

"I had to get him out of sight."

"Now what do we do?"

"Well," Clint said, "I wanted to go and find his partners, but now I don't think I can leave you two alone, so . . ."

"So we'll go with you?"

"No."

"Then what?"

"I smell food."

"We made lunch."

"Then let's eat it and I can think about it."

"I hope Emily can eat, after seeing that man shot."

"I hope you can eat."

"I think so," she said. "I kind of wanted to shoot him myself."

"Can you handle a gun?"

"If I have to."

"That's good to know."

"Then we can come?"

"No," Clint said, "but maybe I can leave you with Emily and a gun and you can protect her."

"But—"

"Why don't I go up and make sure she's all right, and we can have lunch," he said.

"Okay," she said. "I'll bring it out to the dining room."

Clint went upstairs and found Emily sitting on the bed in the front room.

"Is he gone?" she asked.

"Yes, he's gone."

"Did you kill him?"

"Emily—"

"I hope you killed him," she said. "He hurt Kathy."

"He's dead, Emily," he said, "and yes, I killed him."

He walked over and sat down on the bed next to her.

"You and Kathy have made a really good lunch," he said. "Do you want to come down and eat it?"

"Oh yes," she said, "I'm really hungry."

"I mean, I hope seeing me shoot that man—"

"Come on, Clint," she said, bounding off the bed. "Let's go and eat!" She grabbed his hand and tugged him out the door.

They ate lunch—meat loaf with all the vegetables—and the subject of the man with the gun never came up. Over coffee and pie, Kathy and Emily talked about baking cookies later.

Clint thought about the situation, wondered if he dared to leave the two of them alone again—Kathy armed with a rifle—to go and look for the other looters. He wished he'd been able to get more information out of the dead man, but things hadn't worked out that way.

While the girls cleaned up, he took a cup of coffee into the living room and sat down on the couch. There was plenty of the day left, and the other looters might not be expecting to see their partner again until later on. Maybe he could take the chance of leaving Kathy and Emily alone until it started getting dark.

He looked over in the corner, where his rifle leaned against a wall, and wondered if Kathy had any guns of her own in the house.

"Okay," Clint said as Kathy came out of the kitchen, "I think we can take a chance here. I'm going out and scout around, see if I can find the gunman's friends. You and Emily should be safe here for the rest of the day."

"What about his friends missing him?" she asked.

"That probably won't happen until later today," Clint said. "Maybe by then I'll know where they are."

"Are you going to try and stop them from looting the town?" she asked.

"I don't know," he said. "If the town has been abandoned, maybe they're not looting, maybe they're salvaging."

"Is there a difference?"

"Yes," he said, "salvage is legal."

"So what will you do?"

"Locate them, find out what they're doing, see if they're a danger to us."

"Isn't that obvious from what that man did?"

"Maybe it is," he said. "And maybe I should make contact and let them know we're both a danger to them. We just want to be left alone."

"Do you think they'll understand that?"

"I don't know," he said. "I guess that's something I'll have to find out. Do you have a gun in the house?"

"Yes, a Winchester."

"Good," he said. "Keep it with you. I'll be back as soon as I can. Try to keep Emily away from the windows."

"Maybe," Kathy said, "she and I should keep watch out the windows."

"If you hear anybody trying to get into the house," he said, "shoot."

"What if it's you?"

"I'll let you know if it's me," he said. "If you don't see or hear me, then shoot first. Understand?"

"I understand."

"I'm leaving Emily in your hands," he said. "You've got to keep her safe."

"And who keeps you safe?" she asked.

"I've been doing that for myself for years," he said. "Don't worry about me."

"If you don't mind," she said, "I'll just worry until you come back."

"All right," Clint said. "Let me just explain the situation to Emily before I go. I don't want her charging out of the house after me again."

"I'll go and get her," Kathy said, and went into the kitchen.

FIFTEEN

Clint made his way back to the abandoned stockyards, moving slowly. As he approached the building where the loot was stacked, he heard voices. Instead of trying to get a look inside, he stayed close to the walls as he worked his way around to the other side. He saw a buckboard by the open doors of the building. As he watched, a man came out, grabbed a carton off the back of the buckboard, and went back inside. Before long, another man came out, did the same thing. He continued to watch until he realized three men were unloading the buckboard. But that didn't necessarily mean there were only three men inside the building. Now he needed to get a look.

He went around to the side of the building to a window and peered in. From there he couldn't see anything. He moved to another window, and from there he was able to see what was going on. They were still stacking booty in the center of the room. He counted the men and this time he came to four. They were talking but he couldn't hear what they were saying. Being able to hear them would certainly help, so he went to the front—since they were loading in the back—and approached a small door. He tried the handle, found it unlocked, and opened it. He didn't go inside. With the door opened a crack, he could hear the men.

"Benson is missing," one of them said.

"Don't worry about Benson," another man said. "He'll be back later. He's checking out another part of town to see if it's worth looting."

"Yeah," a third man said, "meanwhile he gets out of the grunt work of loading and unloading a wagon."

"We all do our share," a man said. He seemed to be the leader. At least, he was standing aside and watching the other men unload the wagon, while he was supervising at that moment.

"How much longer we gonna be doin' this?" one man asked.

"Until we're done," the supervisor said. "There are a lot of us involved in this, Jakes. We need to have enough to make each of our shares worth it."

"You sure we ain't gonna catch anythin' from this stuff?" another man asked.

"Or just from bein' in this town?"

"Don't worry," the supervisor said. "The doc says we're all safe."

"I don't know," one of the others said. "I ain't been feelin' that good lately."

"You're imaginin' it," the supervisor said. "Just don't worry about it. Keep workin'."

"Yeah, yeah," the other man said, "we'll keep workin'."

"I'll be right back," the supervisor said.

The supervisor was coming out, and Clint didn't know what door he was using, so he closed the door and backed away.

He retreated to some outside stalls, where he could take cover. He was lucky. The door he had been listening at opened and a man stepped out. He was tall, fit, in his forties. He took out some makings, rolled himself a cigarette, and lit it. Then he started to walk . . . stroll, really.

Clint had a choice to make. Stay in hiding, or make a move. Come up behind the man, get the drop on him, and question him. But then what? Let him go, so he could tell the others? Or kill him? Clint wished someone had said the man's name, so he had something to go on. Maybe it would be a name that Kathy knew from town.

The man continued to smoke and walk, then stomped the cigarette out and headed back to the building. Clint had missed the window. He decided to just hang around and see if any other men showed up. Five he might be able to handle—only it was down to four now.

Hopefully.

Clint stayed until it was dusk. The four men did not come out, and no one else went in. He moved closer to see if he could eavesdrop again. He cracked the door and listened.

"Where we gonna eat tonight?" someone asked.

Clint recognized the voice of the supervisor.

"Here," he said. "Make a fire and we'll cook somethin' up."

"Can't we go to one of the cafés, cook somethin' up there?" another man asked.

"No," the boss said, "I wanna wait here for Benson to come back."

"Where is he anyway?"

"I don't know," the boss said. "We might have to go out and look for him."

"If we're gonna do that," somebody said, "maybe we should do it before it gets dark."

"Yeah, you're right," the boss said. "We can eat later. You boys get out there and find him. Maybe he found somebody else in town."

"We ain't found nobody else in town yet," one of the other men said. "What do we do if we do?"

"Anybody left in town who's still alive," the boss said,

"has an accident. We don't need any witnesses. This place isn't officially a ghost town yet."

Clint closed the door, turned, and ran back to the boardinghouse.

SIXTEEN

"Change of plans," Clint said as he entered the house.

"Jesus, Clint!" Kathy said. "I almost shot you. What's going on?"

"The dead man's friends are looking for him," Clint said, "and they're going to kill anyone they find alive in town."

"So what are we gonna do?"

"We have to move."

"Leave my house?" she said. "If I'd wanted to do that, I would've left already."

"It's temporary," he said, "just until I can take care of these men."

"How many are there?" she asked.

"Four, so far," he said. "Look, where's Emily?"

"Upstairs."

"Get her down here, and pack some food. You two have to go into hiding."

"For how long?"

"As long as it takes me to handle the looters."

"But where can we go?" she asked. "Those men are searching the whole town, right?"

"Right," Clint said, "but since the man I killed found

you, I have to assume they will, too. They'll be coming to this area. We just have to get away from here—now!"

"Okay!" Kathy said. "I'll get Emily."

While Kathy went upstairs, Clint walked over and looked out the front windows, then moved to the back of the house and looked out the windows there.

Kathy came down with Emily, who was asking questions.

"Where are we goin', Clint?" Emily called out.

"Not sure, little girl," he said as he returned to the living room, "but we have to leave here, just for a little while."

"I'll get some food," Kathy said, and went to the kitchen.

Clint looked out the front windows again, decided that they better go out the back.

"Okay," he said to Emily, "come on." He took her hand and led her to the kitchen. Kathy was finishing up, sliding some cold chicken into a burlap bag.

"We're going out the back," Clint said, grabbing the sack from her. "Hold on to Emily and stay close."

"Right." Kathy had Emily in one hand and her rifle in the other.

He went out the back door, holding his hand out to stop them. When he saw that the coast was clear, he waved them out.

"We're going to move fast."

"But . . . to where?"

"Just away from here," Clint said. "Then we'll figure out where to go."

They ran to the house next door, where Clint had hidden the body, then to the house after that. Then Clint saw two of the men from the stockyard stable.

"Down!" he said.

They all ducked as the two men walked by.

"Can't you take care of them?" Kathy whispered.

"Not while you and Emily are here," Clint said. "I don't want to take the chance of a stray bullet."

"But I can shoot—" Kathy said.

"You have to protect Emily."

"Right. So where are we going?"

"Someplace they've already been," he said.

"And where's that?"

Clint looked at Emily.

"Emily, where did you see the men before?"

"A few places," she said.

"Just tell me one."

"They were in the Magnolia," the child said. "I hid from them."

Clint looked at Kathy.

"The Magnolia Hotel," she said. "Just off of Main Street."

"Okay, then," Clint said. "Lead us to the Magnolia Hotel."

"This way," Kathy said.

SEVENTEEN

They had to duck out of sight one more time, this time from a single man. After he went past, they continued on to the Magnolia Hotel. They went in the front door without being seen.

"Shouldn't we close the doors?" Kathy asked.

"No," Clint said, "they may have noticed that the doors were open. If we close them, they'll know somebody's inside."

"So we're going to leave the hotel unlocked while we're in here?"

"We'll put you in a room and you can lock that door."

"All right."

Clint went to the front desk, got behind, inspected the keys, and then chose one. He held it up to Kathy and said, "The honeymoon suite okay? It's probably the biggest room in the hotel."

"Sounds good to me."

The Magnolia was a large hotel, fashioned after a Southern mansion, three stories high. The honeymoon suite was on the third floor. They walked up.

"Wow!" Emily said. "What a pretty room."

Although it was a "honeymoon suite," and both a man

and a woman would be using it, the room was decorated all in pink and was wall-to-wall frills.

Clint walked to one of two windows and looked out. The suite looked out over the main street.

"This is a fine view of this part of town," Clint said, "both ways, and the rooftops across the street."

"You want me to keep watch?" Kathy asked.

"I want you to stay away from the window," Clint said. "Every so often, though, have a peek outside and see what's going on. If you hear any noise, take a look. And keep Emily away from the window."

"I can keep watch, too," Emily said.

"I know you can, sweetie," Clint said, "but I really need you to stay away from the windows."

She folded her arms indignantly and said, "Hmph."

Clint looked at Kathy.

"I'll keep her away from the windows," Kathy assured him.

"Okay," Clint said. "I'm going to go out the back and see if I can locate those men again."

"Are you gonna go against them?"

"I'm going to see if I can determine without a doubt how many of them there are," Clint said. "Maybe we can stay hidden long enough for them to pack up and move out."

"You're not going to try to stop them?"

"That's not my job, Kathy," Clint said.

"But . . . you can't just let them take everything," she argued. "What if they decide to go through my house? Take my valuables?"

"What valuables do you have?" Clint asked. "I can go get them for you."

"Well . . . just everything," she said. "everything in the house. That house is all I have, Clint."

"They're not going to take your house," Clint said.

"B-But you can't just stand by while they loot the town," she said.

"Look," Clint said, "first let me scout around and find out how many men we're actually dealing with. Then we can talk about what to do."

"Yes," she said, "well, all right. Okay."

"Emily," Clint said, "I'll be back soon. You do what Kathy tells you to do."

"All right."

"And stay away from the windows, you hear?"

"I hear."

Clint went to the door, looked back at the two of them one more time, then left the suite.

EIGHTEEN

Clint slipped out the back door of the hotel, made his way to Kathy's part of town, keeping to the shadows as it got dark. As he got there, he saw two men outside the house he'd put the body in. They were talking to each other, very animated. Then the door opened and a third man came out—the supervisor. Clint moved closer so he could hear what they were saying . . .

"Somebody plugged him once," the supervisor said.

"We didn't hear no shot," one of the others said.

"Too far away," the boss said. Clint was still waiting to hear his name. He didn't have to wait much longer.

"Steve, what's goin' on?" the second man said. "Who killed Kenny?"

"I don't know," Steve said.

"Well," the first man said, "somebody's in town with us—somebody we ain't seen yet. I don't like it."

"Neither do I," Steve said. "We've gotta find him, though."

"We need more men to search the whole town," one of them said.

"Find Chris, Billy," Steve said. "Me and Ned are gonna

keep searching around here. You two start in another part of town."

"We need more men," Billy said again.

"I'll send for 'em," Steve said. "But let's get started first."

"Okay," Billy said. "What about the little girl?"

"What about her?" Steve asked.

"Well, we know she's in town," Billy said. "We seen her. Maybe she's seen whoever killed Kenny."

"Yeah, well, if you find 'er, you can ask 'er," Steve said. "Now get goin'."

"Yeah, okay," Billy said. He left, walking away from where Clint was hiding so he didn't have to move.

"Okay," Steve said, "you start on that side of the street, I'll take this side. Check all the houses. Start with that big one. I think it used to be a boardinghouse."

"Yeah, okay."

"If you find anybody, don't kill 'im. We'll have to find out who he is or what he wants. Or them."

"You think there's another gang in town?" Ned asked.

"I don't know. But we're gonna find out."

The two men split up. Clint left his hiding place and ran back to the boardinghouse. He wanted to get inside before Ned got there. Ned was going to give him some answers.

NINETEEN

Clint heard the front door open and close, heard the man's footsteps. He wanted to get the drop on him so he wouldn't have to kill him before questioning him.

Clint waited in the kitchen while the man went through the rest of the house. He was starting to think he'd picked the wrong room to hide in. What if Ned decided not to look in the kitchen?

However, several minutes later he heard Ned's footsteps as he approached the kitchen. Clint flattened himself against the wall and took out his gun.

The swinging kitchen door opened and Ned entered. Clint immediately stuck his gun barrel into the small of the man's back.

"Just take it easy," he said. "Don't do anything stupid."

"You killed Kenny," Ned said.

"I did," Clint said. "Right here, in fact. He didn't give me much choice."

"Y-You gonna kill me?"

"I don't plan to," Clint said, taking Ned's gun from his holster. "Not unless you make me."

"Whataya want?"

"Just to talk," Clint said. "Have a seat."

The man walked to the kitchen table and sat down tentatively, as if he didn't believe Clint and was expecting to be shot.

"Who are you fellas?" Clint asked.

"Whataya wanna know for?"

"Your name's Ned. Ned what?"

"Potter."

"And who's Steve, your boss?"

"Steve Harwick."

"I never heard of him. Where's he from?"

"From here. We're all from here."

"Who else?"

"Billy, Kenny—but you killed Kenny."

"Who else?"

"Chris."

"Who else?"

"That's it," Ned said, "Five of us."

"I heard Steve say he could get more men," Clint said. "From where?"

Ned eyed Clint's gun before answering.

"The telegraph office," he said. "Steve knows how to operate the key. He can send for more men."

So the key was still operational. That might have been good news, but for now it was bad.

"So all of you lived here," Clint said. "When the disease drove everyone out, you came back to loot the town. Is that right?"

"Yeah," Ned said. "It was Steve's idea. He said it wasn't illegal because the town was abandoned. You know, like a ghost town."

"Well, I don't know about that exactly," Clint said. "I don't know if ghost towns have to be . . . declared somehow. But I don't know that Steve is right about this being legal. Somehow, though, I don't think he'd care—or that you'd care."

"Hey," Ned said, "who are you anyway? And why ain't you sick?"

"My name is Clint Adams," he said, "and I suspect I'm not sick for the same reason you're not. Somehow I'm immune. Or I just haven't gotten sick yet. I've only been here for a couple of days."

"Clint Adams?" Ned said. "The—Gunsmith?"

"That's right."

"Jesus," Ned said, scooting his chair back a bit, as if he was thinking about running. "W-Who sent you here?"

"Nobody," Clint said. "I just happened to ride in."

"A coincidence?"

Clint made a face. He hated that word, but said, "Yes."

"And now you plan to stop us?" Ned asked.

"Actually," Clint said, "I don't care if you loot the town. I just don't want you to—"

"You've seen the girl," Ned said.

"Yes. I don't want you to hurt her."

"We don't intend to hurt her," Ned said. "We knew she was here, and we left her alone."

"Rather than help her?"

"Steve said we were better off leaving her be," Ned said. "Let her fend for herself. He said that would be helpin' her."

"Where do you and your friends spend the night?"

"We operate out of the stockyards," Ned said. "We just sleep in the stables."

"Are there parts of town you still haven't yet looted?" Clint asked.

"Plenty," Ned said, "but Steve said we'd work about week, and then leave with what we have."

"How will you transport the loot?"

"Steve will send for more men with wagons."

"How many more men does he have?"

"Maybe half a dozen," Ned said. "He hasn't really told us everything."

With half a dozen more, that would make ten altogether. Clint had to try to disable that key before Steve could send a telegraph message.

"Okay," Clint said.

"Okay . . . what? Are you gonna kill me now? Like you did Kenny?"

"I told you, your friend Kenny didn't give me any choice," Clint said. "What about you? You going to give me a choice, Ned?"

"Huh? Oh, yeah, sure," Ned said. "I don't wanna get killed."

"Then you'll do what I say?"

"Sure, sure. Um, whataya want me to do?"

TWENTY

Clint stopped just down the street from the telegraph office. He checked out the street, up and down, not wanting to run into Steve at the telegraph office. Once he was sure he was clear, he made his way down to the office and went inside.

Nothing had changed since he was there last with Emily. The place was still littered with flimsy yellow slips of paper. What he didn't know was whether or not Steve had already been there to send for more men. But he made sure if it hadn't happened already, it wouldn't happen at all. He hated to use the butt of his pistol, but he did so, and smashed the key to bits. Nobody would be sending any messages from this time on.

Clint got out of the telegraph office quickly, and made his way over to the Magnolia Hotel. As he approached it, he looked up and saw someone duck back from the window quickly, allowing the curtain to swing closed.

Damn it.

Clint let himself into the honeymoon suite and found Emily sitting in a chair with her hands folded in her lap, looking very innocent.

"Don't look so innocent," he said to her. "I saw you at the window."

Her eyes widened and she said, "It wasn't me."

"Emily—"

"It wasn't her," Kathy said from across the room, "it was me."

"You?"

"I'm sorry," she said. "I was just trying to keep an eye out, like you said."

"You have to be more careful, Kathy," Clint said. "If somebody sees a curtain swinging, it can give us away."

"I know," she said, "I'm sorry."

"All right, never mind," he said.

"Do you want something to eat?" she asked.

"No, I'm not hungry."

"Did you find out anything?"

"I found out . . . a bit," he said, hesitating and looking at Emily.

"You might as well talk in front of her," she said. "Emily has a right to know what's going on. After all, she saw you shoot that man."

"Ka-blam!" Emily said, making a gun of her hand.

"Shooting a man is not funny, Emily," Clint said.

She lowered her hand and her chin.

"So, what did you find out?"

He told her about finding Ned in her house, and what he did to the telegraph key.

"But won't we need that key?" she asked.

"I don't know how to operate a telegraph key, do you?" he asked.

"Well, no . . ."

"And I don't want them using it, so . . ."

"What about that other man?" she asked. "Ned? Did you kill him and leave his body in my house?"

"No," Clint said, "I didn't kill him, and I didn't leave him in your house. I took him to the other house—where I left the other man's body—and left him tied up."

"Why that house?"

"Because they already found Kenny's body," Clint said. "So it may be a while before they find Ned. Besides, I put him in a closet."

"So what do we do now?" she asked.

"Well, I damaged the telegraph key, but I don't know if the boss, Steve, already sent a message or not. If he did, then I have to take care of these four men before six more show up."

"And how will you do that?"

"The easiest way to do it would be one at a time."

TWENTY-ONE

In the morning Clint once again left Kathy and Emily at the Magnolia after a cold breakfast together. He went downstairs and left by the back door. With Ned tied up in a closet, he had three men to deal with. If he could isolate them and take them out one at a time, that would be ideal. If he had to face all three at once . . . well, he'd hate for it to come to that, since he had no idea of how good they were with their guns.

But before he could determine any of that, he had to find them again.

"Whataya mean, he's gone?" Billy asked. "Gone where?"

"I don't know," Steve said. "He went to check on the rooming house, and I ain't seen him since."

"So he's dead, too?" Chris asked.

"We don't know that," Steve said. "Maybe he's still out there lookin'. Maybe he slept somewhere else."

"Why would he do that?" Chris asked. "We all been sleepin' in that barn."

They were in a small saloon not far from the stockyards, sitting at a table with a bottle of whiskey in front of them, and four glasses—only three of which had the amber liquid in them. They were washing down their breakfast of beef jerky.

"So now we gotta go out and look for Ned?"

"You two do that," Steve said. "And stay together."

"What about you?"

"I'm gonna go send another telegram."

"I thought you sent for help already," Chris said.

"I did," Steve said, "but maybe we need more. We'll meet back here in half an hour."

"Okay," Billy said.

They all finished their drinks, then left the bottle on the table and walked out of the saloon together. In front they split up.

Clint went back to the stockyards to try to pick up the trail again, but none of the men were there. He looked around, keeping out of sight as much as possible, and finally decided to go back to the area where the boardinghouse was. He wanted to see if Ned was still tied up in the closet. If he wasn't, that meant there were four men out there searching for him.

Steve Harwick walked into the telegraph office and immediately noticed the condition of the key. Smashed. Well, that cinched it. Somebody was in town, and was hoping to isolate them. At least he got one message out, and before long, there'd be six more men joining them in the search. He just wished he knew how many men they were dealing with.

Then he thought about the little girl. It might do them some good to have her in hand. If it came to it, they could use her as a hostage.

He left the telegraph office and went in search of the little girl.

Billy and Chris searched for Ned, and neither of them was very happy.

"I don't like this," Chris said. "Somebody's pickin' us off one by one."

"That's why you and me are stayin' together," Billy said. "Ain't nobody pickin' us off."

"You can say that again!" Chris agreed.

Billy put his hand on his gun and said, "Ain't nobody gettin' close to us!"

Chris touched his own gun and added, "Not without gettin' their heads blown off!"

TWENTY-TWO

Clint spotted the two men at the south end of town, where he himself had not spent much time—which was actually the reason he decided to look there. There were businesses up and down the street, but the buildings here were older, some of them in disrepair.

He decided rather than bracing the two men, he'd tail them close enough to eavesdrop on them. Maybe he could collect some information that way.

Clint heard the two men bitching about being picked off, and promising each other they'd stay together. Nothing very interesting, but then the subject changed to their boss.

"What about Steve?" Chris asked.

"Steve Harwick can take care of hisself, believe me," Billy said. "Maybe he don't got the big reputation, but I seen him handle a gun. He's fast! I seen him outdraw three men one time."

"Three?"

"Killed 'em all."

"Damn. That's the kinda thing that does build a rep. Why ain't he got one?"

"'Cause he don't care about that stuff," Billy said. "He

cares about makin' money, though, which is why he come up with this plan."

"This part of town ain't so good," Chris said. "We ain't gonna work this end, are we?"

"That's up to Steve, but I doubt it," Billy said. "It would take too much time, and it sure don't look like it'd be worth it."

"Then what would Ned be doin' here?" Chris argued. "Why we lookin' here?"

"Because we gotta look everywhere, that's why," Billy said. "Ain't no point in not findin' him just 'cause we decided not to look here. Come on, it ain't gonna take that long."

"Yeah, okay . . ."

Clint fell back, satisfied with what he had heard. Steve Harwick sounded like a smart man, and a smart man who was also good with a gun was dangerous. Maybe he ought to take these two out while he could, leaving Harwick alone—unless he had already called for help.

Clint worked to catch up to the two men again, to see if they'd reveal anything else.

"I can hit what I shoot at, but I ain't no fast gun," Billy was telling Chris. "What about you?"

"I ain't never shot at another man," Chris said. He appeared to be about ten years younger than the other men.

"Well, you will someday," Billy said. "Might as well be now."

"Yeah, but there's only three of us—"

"Right now," Billy said, cutting him off. "But you heard Steve. He's already sent a message to get us six more men to help load and transport. So they might as well help us hunt, too."

"Well," Chris said, "with that many men and guns, maybe I won't have to kill anybody."

"Maybe not, if there's only one man in town pickin' us

off," Billy said, "but if there's more, you better do your part, boy."

"Don't worry, Billy," Chris said. "I'll do my part."

"You better, if you want to get a full share," Billy explained.

"I will," Chris said, "I swear."

"Okay," Billy said. "Okay, look, you cross the street and we'll cover both sides at once."

"B-But . . . Steve told us to stay together."

"Yeah, well, we'll just be across the street from each other. We'll be able to see each other."

"I don't know—"

"Come on, kid," Billy said. "We'll finish up faster that way."

"Yeah, okay," Chris said. "But you keep your eye on me."

"And you keep your eye on me."

"Agreed."

Chris nodded, and started across the street . . .

Very quickly, Clint made up his mind. He fell back, crossed the street, and took up a position in one of the empty businesses. All he had to do was wait for young Chris to come along and stick his head inside. Once he took him out, the other fellow—Billy—might just come running to see what happened to his partner.

This was Clint's opportunity to cut the odds down from three-to-one to even money.

TWENTY-THREE

Billy Cabot walked from doorway to doorway, sticking his head in, looking the place over, then stepping out and looking across the street to check on Chris, who was doing the same on his side of the street.

Chris Hunter was more tentative each time he stuck his head in a door, as if he was expecting to get it chopped off. Then he'd withdraw and look across the street for Billy, to make sure he was still there.

Clint watched silently as Billy moved along, figuring Chris was right with him on his side of the street. Then he heard the sound of Chris's boots on the boardwalk as he approached the store he was hidden in. He moved away from the window to the door.

Chris's footsteps came right up to the door. When the young man stuck his head in, Clint reached out and grabbed him, yanked him into the store. As the boy went by him, he snatched his gun from his holster so fast that Chris didn't realize it was gone. He turned and reached for it. Only then did he realize it was missing.

"What the—"

"Quiet, boy," Clint said, pointing Chris's own gun at him.

Chris looked at the barrel of the gun and swallowed hard.

"Keep your voice down," Clint said.

"W-Who are you?"

"My name's Clint Adams."

The boy's eyes went wide.

"The Gunsmith?"

"That's right."

"What're you doin' here?"

"Right now I'm trying to keep from killing you," Clint said. "You want to help me with that?"

"What?"

Clint spoke more slowly.

"Do you want to help me not kill you?"

"Well . . . sure," Chris said. "I don't wanna get killed."

"Good," Clint said. "You and me are going to wait until your friend across the street notices you're gone."

"Then what?"

"Then he'll come looking for you, and I'll take his gun, too."

"You won't get Billy's gun as easy as you got mine."

"We'll see. Let's watch."

Clint moved Chris over to the window and they both looked out.

Billy checked the last building on his side, then turned to look across the street. He didn't see Chris, so he assumed the boy had gone into one of the buildings. He waited for him to come out, and waited, and waited . . .

When Chris didn't reappear, Billy froze. Something was wrong. Whoever was picking them off one by one had done it again. Chris was gone.

Billy went into the street, the first step toward crossing over to look for the boy, but he abruptly changed his mind. He backed up onto the boardwalk, turned, and hurried away.

* * *

"What's he doin'?" Chris demanded.

"What's it look like he's doing, boy?" Clint asked.

"He's . . . he's leavin'," Chris said. "He ain't comin' lookin' for me."

"No, he's not."

Clint turned away from the window, kept his eyes on the boy so he wouldn't try anything. But Chris was beyond that. He was devastated by the fact that his colleague, his partner Billy, was walking away without trying to find him.

"Where's he goin'?" Chris asked, aloud.

"He's going to find your boss," Clint said. "Steve."

"What—what are you gonna do with me?"

"The same thing I did to your friend Ned," Clint said.

"Did you kill him?"

"No," Clint said. "You see where we are?"

Chris looked around.

"A hardware store."

"Right," Clint said. "Come on, we're going to find some rope."

A little while later, Chris was gagged and securely tied, hands and feet, and placed in the back room of the hardware store. Clint even piled some crates around him, to hide him from sight. Then Clint left the store.

He had successfully cut the odds down to two-to-one.

Or so he thought.

TWENTY-FOUR

Steve Harwick decided to look for Ned someplace the others might not have gone. He went back to the house where they'd found Kenny's body. If he was going to hide another body, that's where he would put it.

He entered the house, checked to see if Kenny was still there. He was, and he was only just starting to smell bad. Steve went through the rest of the house, and when he got to one of the bedrooms, he heard a noise coming from the closet. He went to the door and found it locked. There was no key. He looked around the room, found a key on a dresser top, and tried it. It unlocked the door. He swung it open and looked down at Ned, hands and feet tied, gagged, thumping his heels on the floor. Because the closet was so small, that was all he could do.

Steve reached down, dragged Ned out of the closet, and then untied him.

"What happened?" he demanded.

"I got jumped in that boardinghouse," Ned said, trying to straighten his legs but finding it painful.

"By who?" Steve asked. "How many men?"

"Just one man," Ned said, "the one who killed Kenny."

"You let one man take you?" Steve said. "Who the hell was it?"

"Steve," Ned said, "it was Clint Adams."

"Adams?" Steve asked. "What the hell is the Gunsmith doing in Medicine Bow?"

"Taking us one at a time," Ned said. "First Kenny, then me. I don't know who's next."

"Why didn't he kill you, Ned?" Steve asked. "Why kill Kenny and not you?"

"He said Kenny didn't give him no choice," Ned said. "I did. I chose to stay alive. See, I figured you'd find me."

"You did, huh?"

"Well, you found me, didn't ya?"

"Yeah, I did."

"What, you think I'm in on it with him? What was I doing trussed up in a closet?"

"Okay," Steve said, reaching his hand out, "come on, get up."

He grabbed Ned's hand and hauled him to his feet. Ned hobbled about, trying to get the feeling back into his legs and arms.

"Where are the others?" he asked.

"Out lookin' for you," Steve said. "Come on, we'll go find them, and then we're gonna find that girl."

Outside Ned asked, "You got more men comin'?"

"I do," Steve said. "Six. They should be here tonight."

"We gotta stay alive 'til then," Ned said.

"Don't worry about that," Steve said. "We'll just stay together."

"You're pretty fast, Steve," Ned said. "You think you can take the Gunsmith?"

"I don't know," Steve said, "and I ain't anxious to try."

"Why?" Ned asked. "Killin' the Gunsmith would give you a big reputation."

"I don't want a reputation, Ned," Steve said. "I just wanna

be rich. No, if we have to face the Gunsmith, we're gonna face him together. All of us."

Clint had questioned Chris before gagging him, and the boy had been so distraught he had talked. He said that all along Steve had been saying that they were to leave the little girl alone. That they could always find her later and use her, if they had to.

Clint figured once Steve realized he was losing his men one by one, he'd look for Emily. And now that Kenny was dead, and Ned and Chris were missing, he had to know something was up.

Clint headed for the Magnolia Hotel in a rush, still careful to keep out of sight.

Along the way he almost ran headlong into two men. He took cover, and recognized them as they went by. Steve and . . . Ned! Obviously Steve had thought to look in the house where Clint had left Kenny's body, and had freed Ned. Now Clint's two-to-one odds were back up to three-to-one. He almost decided to step out and brace them while there were only two, but then he thought about Emily and Kathy. What would they do if he became careless and got himself killed?

So he let them go by, waited for them to get out of sight, and then ran for the Magnolia.

Steve and Ned saw Billy running toward them.

"What the hell—" Ned said. "He looks like he seed a ghost."

"Ned!" Billy said. "You're alive."

"Sure, I'm alive," Ned said. "Steve found me."

"Where the hell have you been?" Steve asked. "What happened? Where's Chris?"

"He's gone!"

"Whataya mean, gone?" Steve asked.

"I mean one minute he was there, and then he wasn't," Billy said. "I guess they got him, too."

"There's no they," Steve said. "It's one man, according to Ned."

"One man?" Billy looked to Ned for confirmation.

"Clint Adams."

Billy's eyes went even wider.

"The goddamned Gunsmith?"

Ned nodded.

"What the hell is he doin' here?"

"He said he was just passin' through."

"Goddamn!" Billy said. "That's a bad coincidence, Steve."

"Yeah, it is. Come on."

"Where we goin'?" Billy asked.

"You're gonna show us where you saw Chris last," Steve said. "If he left Ned alive, maybe he did the same thing to Chris. Probably tied him up and left him someplace, too."

"We find him, we'll be back to four," Ned said.

"Four of us?" Billy asked. "Against the Gunsmith?"

"There are more comin'," Steve said. "Six. They'll be here by tonight."

"So why don't we just wait for them to get here?" Billy asked. "I mean, find a hole and wait?"

"Because," Steve said, "it's better to be the hunter than the hunted. If we just hide, Adams will be out there hunting us. But if we hunt him, maybe he'll go into hiding. He doesn't know we've got six more men coming. Once they get here, we'll have him hopelessly outnumbered."

"What about just leavin'?" Ned asked. "We got plenty of stuff. Let's just go when the other men get here."

"Not my call," Steve said. While he was their boss, he wasn't the man in charge of the whole show, even though he'd had a lot to do with the planning. "And I can't send any more telegrams, so we'll just have to stick to our plan to pick this town clean."

"So right now we're lookin' for the Gunsmith?" Ned asked. "That don't seem like the smartest thing for anybody to do, ya know?"

"Right now we're lookin' for Chris," Steve corrected. "When we have four men again, then we'll start lookin' for the Gunsmith . . . and we'll all stick together."

"That suits me," Billy said.

"Me, too," Ned said. "I ain't lookin' to face the Gunsmith alone again. I thought he was gonna kill me."

TWENTY-FIVE

When Clint got back to the Magnolia, Kathy and Emily were sitting together on one of the beds. Between them was a deck of cards. Clint didn't know what game they were playing, but it didn't matter.

"Pack up," he said. "We're moving again."

"But why?"

Clint looked at Emily, who was still frowning at the cards in front of her, and said to Kathy, "I'll tell you later."

Kathy got off the bed and started packing.

"But where are we going?"

"I've thought about it," Clint said. "I think we need to go someplace they won't think to look."

"And where's that?"

"Someplace they've already been."

"Where is that?" Kathy asked.

"I don't know," Clint said. "Maybe back to your house."

"That would suit me," she said.

Clint drew her aside while Emily remained on the bed. He quickly told her everything that had happened, and what he had heard.

"There's a good chance they'll find the boy I left tied up, too," he finished.

"So there'll be four of them again," she said. "I suppose that means you should have killed the two men stead of tying them up."

"I only kill when someone is trying to kill me," he said. "Both of those men were helpless."

"But . . . they'll be looking for you now? To kill you, right?"

"Right."

"And Emily."

He nodded.

"The only person they're not looking for," he said, "is you."

"Only because they don't know about me."

"Can you ride?" he asked her.

"Well, yes, of course I can ride, but I'm sure my horse is gone, taken along when they all left town."

"That's probably true," Clint said, "but if I can find you a horse . . ."

"You expect me to leave you and Emily here?"

"Not Emily," he said. "If I can get you one horse, you can ride out of here with her."

"And what about you?" she asked. "You have a horse. You could leave with Emily."

"No, I can't leave," he said.

"Well, if you can get a horse—and I presume you intend to steal one of theirs—we could all leave."

"Wrong again," he said. "We still don't know if I'm carrying any part of the disease. I can't leave and take a chance of spreading it. But you and Emily have been through it and have come out the other side."

"But where do we go?"

"To the nearest town," he said. "We'll figure that part out. First let's get out of here to someplace less obvious—and hopefully, safer. Get Emily ready."

He went to the front window and looked down at the street. It was empty, but they'd still go out the back.

"We're ready," Kathy said.

"We weren't finished playing," Emily complained.

"Where are we going?" Kathy asked.

"I'm hungry," Emily said.

Clint turned to face the two of them. He was at a great disadvantage as long as he had to worry about them. In the end, they might all end up getting killed.

"We've got to get you out of town," he said. "So we're going to go and find a horse."

"Why can't we just ride Eclipse?" Emily asked.

Why not, indeed? Clint thought.

TWENTY-SIX

Stuart Brock turned the girl over onto her back and stared down at her. Her big breasts leaned to the sides, the areolas slightly elongated. He leaned down and took one nipple into his mouth, and then the other, sucked them both until they were hard.

"Mmmm," she said, "nice."

"Shhh," he told her. "I'm paying you to fuck, not talk."

"But—"

He reared up and smacked her across the face, then held his forefinger to his lips and said, "Shhh," again. This time she remained quiet.

He went back to chewing on her nipples, and did so until the skin was sore and cracked. Then he reached between her legs, but found her dry. He inserted his fingers and manipulated her until she was wet. Then he spread her legs and drove his hard penis into her. He slammed himself in and out of her so hard the bed began to hop up and down. When he was finally ready to explode, he pulled out and let his stream go onto her face and chest. She closed her eyes, but didn't dare make a move to wipe the sticky substance away, for fear of being hit again.

He got off the bed after wiping himself on the sheet, and walked to the door.

"Hale!" he shouted when he opened it.

A man immediately appeared outside the door.

"Yes, sir?"

"Pay her off and escort her out."

"Yes, sir."

"Don't ever bring her back," Brock said. "She spoke."

"I warned her, sir—"

"Never mind," Brock said. "Just get rid of her."

Brock left the room and walked down the hall to another. In anticipation, his servant had already drawn him a hot bath.

He got into the bath and settled down into the hot water. Hale appeared with a cigar, stuck it in Brock's mouth, and lit it.

"Is she gone?"

"Yes, sir."

"Any telegrams?"

"Yes, sir. He's asked for six men and wagons."

"Six?"

"Yes, sir."

"Did you send them?"

"Yes, sir."

"Good," Brock said, letting his head loll back. "How much time do they need?"

"They still need the better part of a week to finish up, sir," Hale said.

"Everything better be going smoothly."

"What could be wrong, sir?" Hale asked. "Everyone thinks the town is diseased."

Brock took a moment to think before asking the next question.

"We did tell him to put up a quarantine sign, didn't we?" Brock asked.

"We told him, sir."

"Meaning?"

Hale firmed his jaw.

"Permission to speak freely, sir."

"Granted."

"I wouldn't be surprised if he forgot."

"And if he forgot, somebody could have ridden into town," Brock said.

"Yes, sir."

Hale took the cigar from Brock's mouth, waited while his boss expelled a long stream of smoke, and then put it back.

"Ah, well," he said, "what harm could a drifter or two do?" Brock asked.

TWENTY-SEVEN

Clint would have to stash Kathy and Emily somewhere safe while he tried to find them a horse. If he couldn't do that, then he'd have to consider letting them ride out on Eclipse.

Actually, having them ride Eclipse would be more up to the horse than up to Clint. The big gelding was particular about who rode him. So far he'd allowed Emily to sit on his back. That didn't mean he'd do the same for Kathy.

"Wait a minute," he said, looking up at the back of a brick building they were passing. "What building is this?"

Kathy looked up and said, "It looks like the back of city hall."

"City hall," Clint said. "There's nothing to loot in city hall. No bank, no county clerk's office, no assessor that I saw when I was in there."

"The mayor's office," Kathy said, "and the town council meets there. The district attorney's office and the courtroom."

"Okay," Clint said, "okay. You two are going to wait for me in here."

"In city hall?" Emily asked. "The mayor's office again?"

"Sure," Clint said, "the mayor's office. Come on, let's find the back door."

Clint forced the back door without much trouble, and

they went up the back stairs. He was carrying the sack of supplies Kathy had packed, and Kathy was carrying her rifle.

Clint was suddenly worried about Eclipse. The horse had been alone in that livery for a long time. He hadn't heard anything during his bouts of eavesdropping to indicate that anyone had found him, but how long would that last? He was going to have to check on him, and move him.

"Now you two stay here," he said as they entered the mayor's office. He put the sack on the desk. "I'll be back soon."

"With a horse?" Kathy asked.

"Hopefully."

"Are you going to bring Eclipse?" Emily asked.

"Maybe I will," Clint said. "Just do what Kathy tells you, honey. Okay?"

"Okay, Clint."

He looked at Kathy.

"Unless you hear my voice," he said, "you shoot anybody who comes through that door, you hear?"

"I hear."

He walked to the door, said, "Lock it," and went out.

It was a miracle, but Eclipse was right where he'd left him. He checked the ground for fresh tracks, but there were none. Apparently, they had decided against using this place for keeping their horses. Was that why that one man had been here? The one whose tracks he'd followed? To check it out?

The gang was probably keeping their horses close to them, in the stockyards. But before Clint went there, he needed to make sure Eclipse was safe. And where was a safe place to put the big gelding?

"Okay, where'd you see him last?" Steve asked Ned.

"Over there," Ned said.

"Where?"

"In front of that hardware store."

"Did he go inside?"

"I don't know."

"Okay," Steve said, "come on. We're all gonna have a look-see."

They crossed the street.

"Kathy! It's me," Clint said at the door to the mayor's office.

"Come on in."

He entered.

"You're back already?" she asked. "Did you find their horses?"

"No," he said, "I had to find a safe place to put my horse first."

"And where is that?"

"Here," Clint said. "He's downstairs in one of the court-rooms."

"Eclipse is here?" Emily asked, clapping her hands. "Can I see him?"

"When I come back," Clint said. "For now you have to stay up here." He looked at Kathy. "I just wanted you to know in case you heard some noise."

He went to the door, said, "Lock it," again, and left.

He made his way to the stockyards, figuring none of the gang would be there. They'd be out looking for him. Or for Chris. Or for both of them.

"Look around," Steve said.

"Where?" Billy asked.

"Everywhere!"

While Billy and Ned looked around in front of the hardware store, Steve went to the storeroom. He walked around, looked in the corners, then thought he heard something. He stopped, and listened. It seemed to be coming from behind some wooden crates that were piled in the middle of the room. Why would they be piled up like that?

"You guys get in here!" he called.

Billy and Ned came running.

"What is it, boss?" Ned asked.

"Move these crates," Steve said.

"Move 'em where?" Billy asked.

"Just move them," Steve said. "I wanna see what's hidden behind them."

Ned and Billy started moving crates, and before long they saw Chris lying there, tied hand and foot.

"Okay," Steve said, "get him untied and up on his feet. Now we're back to four."

TWENTY-EIGHT

Clint found the horses. Five of them. They were in a stable in the rear of the stockyards. Five saddle mounts and five saddles. But there were also four other horses, and two buckboards. Not enough to carry away all of the loot the gang was collecting.

Once again he thought about the telegraph key. Had Steve sent a message before he disabled it? Were there more men and wagons on the way? And if so, how long would it take them to get there?

He quickly saddled one of the horses and walked it outside. He was going to have to be damn lucky to walk the horse to city hall without being seen. He made the walk with his hand on his gun, waiting for someone to shout, or start shooting. But it didn't happen.

When he got to city hall, he walked the horse right in, as he had done with Eclipse, put it in the same room with the big gelding. Then he went upstairs.

"Damn, my legs are asleep," Chris complained, flexing his legs.

"I know just how you feel," Ned said, sympathizing with the kid.

"Chris," Steve said, "what did you tell Adams?"

"Whataya mean?" Chris asked. "I didn't tell him nothin'. Why would I?"

"Come on, kid," Steve said. "We're talkin' about the Gunsmith here. You must've been scared to goddamned death. When he asked you some questions, you answered him. What did you tell him?"

"I just told him . . ." Chris started to say, but allowed his voice to trail off. He was obviously afraid to answer Steve's questions.

"How many of us there are?"

"Well, yeah . . ."

"And did you tell him I was sending for more men?" Steve asked.

"I said . . . yeah, well, that eventually you would be, ya know?"

"You tell him how many?"

"No, no . . . I don't know . . . I mean, I don't know how many you were gonna send for, do I?"

"No, you don't."

"What else did you tell him?" Ned asked. "Did you tell him where our horses are?"

"Shit," Billy said, "the horses."

"All right," Steve said, "okay, we're gonna go and check on the horses. If he didn't move 'em, we're gonna make 'em safe, and then we're gonna go out and find ourselves a Gunsmith."

"What? We're gonna look for him?" Chris said.

"We're gonna look for him and kill him," Steve said. "Ned, where'd you see that little girl?"

"A couple of times near this café on Main Street," Ned said, "one time across from the Magnolia."

"Okay," Steve said, "we're gonna look for her, too. If we threaten her, maybe Adams will come out of hiding."

"You think so?" Ned asked. "He's gonna come out and let us kill him, just to save some little girl he don't know?"

"That's what we're gonna find out," Steve said.

"Boss, I'm sorry—" Chris said.

"Don't worry about it, kid."

"You ain't gonna kill me?"

"No, I'm not gonna kill you," Steve told him. "We need your gun. Come on, let's go."

They left the hardware store and started back to the stockyards to check on their horses. He wouldn't kill the kid until this was all over.

TWENTY-NINE

"You mean leave now?" Kathy asked.

"Right now," Clint said. "Let's go."

"But . . . are you sure you won't come, too?"

"We went over this," Clint said. "I can't leave until I'm sure I won't infect anybody. Now come on."

He hurried them downstairs to where the horses were.

"Can't we take Eclipse?" Emily asked.

"Sorry, sweetie," Clint said. "This is your horse."

She made a face and folded her arms across her chest.

"Don't we need supplies?" Kathy asked.

"You're not riding far," Clint said. "Just to the next town. When you get there, go and talk to the sheriff and tell him what's going on."

"But . . . what town?"

"I passed the town of Givens about thirty miles back," Clint said. "What's the next town going east?"

"I think it's . . . Flint."

"Haw far?"

"I don't know," she said. "Forty miles?"

"Then when the folks left town altogether, they probably went to Givens, right?"

"But you just said you rode through Givens on the way here."

"You're right," he said, shaking his head. What was he thinking? He'd been in Givens and hadn't heard anything about a mass exodus from Medicine Bow. That meant they probably went to Flint.

"Then you'll ride to Flint."

"What if they see us?"

"We'll have to hope they don't," he said. "Come on, we'll go out the back."

"My horse is missing!" Chris exclaimed as they entered the livery.

"And Kenny's saddle," Ned pointed out.

"Why would he need to take one horse?" Steve wondered aloud. "He'd have his own."

"Maybe it's lame," Billy said.

"Maybe he needs one for the little girl," Ned suggested.

"A little girl can't ride on her own," Steve said.

"So then his horse is lame," Billy said.

"Or," Steve said, "he needs it for somebody else."

"Another person?" Chris asked. "So our odds are down."

"Still two-to-one," Ned said, "if that other person can even shoot."

"Maybe they're gonna leave town," Billy said. "Would that be so bad?"

"We can't let 'em leave town," Steve said. "They might go to the law in the next town."

"I thought you said what we were doin' wasn't illegal," Chris said.

"I don't think it is," Steve said, "but I don't want to have to argue the point with a lawman."

Ned and Billy thought Chris was stupid if he didn't know what they were doing was illegal. Why else would they want to kill to keep it a secret?

"Okay," Steve told them, "first we've got to move these horses."

"What about my horse?" Chris asked.

"You can have Kenny's."

"But my horse was better—"

"We'll get it back," Steve said, "after we kill the Gunsmith. But for now we've got to make sure he doesn't get to these animals."

"Why didn't he just take them while he was here?" Billy asked.

"Maybe he couldn't handle five horses," Steve said. "He probably wanted to make some time."

"He could have scattered them."

"That would have attracted attention."

They each grabbed a horse and their saddles—Chris taking Kenny's horse while grumbling about it—and walked them outside.

"Where we gonna take them?" Ned asked.

"We'll find a place," Steve said. "But let's make it quick. We've got to stop him before he puts Chris's horse to use."

"There's a few other stables," Billy said.

"No stable," Steve said. "Someplace he wouldn't think to look."

They all thought a moment, and then Steve said, "I've got it. The jail is big enough."

"The jail?" Chris asked.

"Why not? I don't think he'd look there. Come on. We can walk them so we don't attract too much attention."

"What if he's watchin' us right now?" Chris asked.

"Then it won't make a difference."

"Too bad none of us can track," Ned said. "Or we'd be able to follow him to where he took the horse."

"Forget it," Steve said. None of them had that talent. "Let's just get these horses stashed away and then find him, or the little girl."

THIRTY

They walked the horse out the back door, where Clint gave Kathy a boost up into the saddle. He then lifted Emily up to sit behind her.

"Forty miles," Clint said. "This horse is fit. Should take you four or five hours if you ride straight through. If Emily can stand it."

"Don't worry," she said. "We'll make it, and send back help."

"I want you to ride out the east end of town, and then circle around," Clint said.

"Why not just ride west?"

"It's shorter this way," Clint said. "Less chance of being seen."

"All right."

"Emily," Clint said, "you hold on tight to Kathy, all right?"

"Yes, Clint."

"And I'll see you soon."

Emily wrapped her arms around Kathy and pressed her face to her back.

"Go!" Clint said.

* * *

As much as Clint Adams hated the word "coincidence," it did rear its ugly head from time to time—usually at the wrong time.

Just as Kathy came out from an alley on horseback, with Emily behind her, Steve Harwick and his three men were walking down Main Street.

"What the hell—" Ned said.

"Who's that?" Billy said.

"Never mind who it is," Steve said. "Stop her!"

They all drew their guns.

"Don't hit the little girl," Steve said. "Just keep them from leaving town."

"Right," Ned said, and they all began firing.

Kathy heard the gunfire, and her heart leaped into her throat.

"Hold on, honey!" she said.

"They're shooting at us!" Emily screamed. Her grip on Kathy's waist tightened.

Kathy didn't know what to do, and the horse started to panic.

She froze.

Clint was inside city hall when he heard the shots.

"Damn it!" he swore.

He rushed to the front doors and swung them open. As he stepped out, he saw four men at one end of the street, carrying guns. At the other end, Kathy and Emily were on their horse. He was closer to them than he was to the four gunmen, so he made a snap decision.

He stepped out into the street, drew his gun, and shouted, "Kathy! Here!"

Kathy saw Clint, saw the open front doors of city hall, and knew what she had to do. She wheeled the horse around and kicked it with her heels.

* * *

Steve Harwick saw the man come out of city hall and step into the street.

"That's gotta be Adams," he called out. "Get 'im!"

The four of them turned their attention—and their guns—toward him.

Clint laid down covering fire for Kathy as she rode the horse back toward him. Mostly he was making noise to scatter the four men. Kathy rode the horse right past him and into city hall. Clint then backed into the building and slammed the doors shut.

He turned and helped both Kathy and Emily down from the horse.

"Now what?" Kathy asked.

"Now get your rifle," he said. "We have to keep those fellas out of here."

Harwick and his men fired at Clint, but when the Gunsmith began to fire back, they scattered for cover. As soon as he backed into city hall and closed the door, they came out into the open again.

"Now we have him," Steve said.

"Yeah," Ned said, "but he's in that building. How do we get him out without getting killed?"

"Well," Steve said, "we have several options that might work, before we try the one that definitely will work."

"Which one is that?" Ned asked.

"Burning them out."

THIRTY-ONE

"What do we do?" Kathy asked.

"First we have to barricade the back door," Clint said. "Go to that window and keep an eye out. If they start to come close, fire at them. I'll be right back."

"But—"

"It'll be all right," he assured her. "They'll take some time deciding what to do."

"Clint!" she called as he started away.

"What?"

"Can they get in by way of the roof?"

"This is the tallest building on this side of the street," he said. "That's not an option. Watch that window."

"Okay."

Clint rushed to the back door, looked around for something to block it with. He tried a couple of rooms, found a piece of furniture he thought would do the trick. It was a small wooden bookcase that fit snugly in the hall. Once it was in front of the door, the door could not be opened.

He went back to the front hall. Emily was sitting on the stairs with her face in her hands, her elbows on her knees.

"Are you all right?" he asked.

"I wanted to go for a ride," she said.

"I know you did," he said, "and you will, it'll just be . . . later."

He stopped, took a step back, and saw that there was a small space beneath the stairs.

"Emily?"

"Yes?"

"Come here, please."

She came down the steps and stood in front of him.

"Were you scared when those men were shooting?" he asked.

She hesitated, then said, "Yes."

"Well, they may start shooting again," Clint explained. "I want you to get under here. If they start shooting again, you'll be safe. You won't have to be afraid."

She stepped forward and looked under the steps.

"It'll be like a cave," she said. "My own special cave."

"That's right."

She started to get under, then stopped and looked up at him.

"But I'll still be afraid that you or Kathy will get shot. Is that all right?"

"That's fine, honey," he said. "That's just fine."

She nodded and got under the steps.

"What do we do now?" Ned asked.

"Take Chris and go around back," Steve said. "Find the back door, see if you can get in."

"And if we can?"

"Fire two shots and go in. If you do that, we'll hit the front door."

"And if the back door is locked?"

"Check the back thoroughly," Steve said. "See if there's a window we can use to get in."

"And if there is?"

"Come back here and tell me," Steve said, "and then we'll make plans."

"Okay," Ned said. "Let's go, kid."

As they crossed the street and moved up the alley next to city hall, Billy said, "What do we do?"

"I'm gonna wait here," Steve said. "You go and get all of our rifles."

"Okay."

"Then we'll trying ventilatin' city hall a bit and see how the Gunsmith reacts to that."

Billy turned and ran. Steve Harwick rubbed his jaw and studied the front of city hall.

"What do you see?" Clint asked Kathy.

"There's only one man out there," she said. "The other three left."

"How?"

"What?"

"How did they leave? Separately? Together?"

"Two of them left together, and the third one went off on his own."

"He sent them off to do jobs," Clint said.

"What jobs?"

"They're probably going to try the back door," Clint said. "I'll go back there and check, make sure they don't come in a window. In fact, maybe I'll barricade the windows."

"With what?"

"This building's got to be filled with furniture."

"And what do I do?"

"Same as before," Clint said. "Watch the street. If you see anything that makes you nervous, start shooting."

"Do I shoot to . . . um . . ."

"You shoot to kill, Kathy," Clint said. "If you give them the chance, they'll kill you."

"A-All right."

"Can you do that?"

"I'll do it," she promised.

"I'll be as quick as I can," he promised, and hoped that he would be quick enough.

THIRTY-TWO

Whoever had designed the city hall building had done so with a minimum of windows. The main floor courtroom had none, and most of the windows that were in the buildings were on the upper floors.

Clint went to the back door to watch and make sure it would hold. Somebody jiggled the doorknob, found it locked, but did not try to force the door. He peered in a back window, but Clint cut down his view by shoving a large hutch into the way.

He went around the main floor and moved furniture, covering the windows as best he could with sofas, desks, bookshelves, anything he could lean against them. Some of the items would not keep out anyone who was bound and determined to enter, but they'd make a hell of a lot of noise doing it.

He hurried back to the front hall.

"Anything?"

"One of the men came back, carrying four rifles. Then the other two came back, so now they all have rifles."

"They might start pumping lead into here at any moment," Clint said. "When they do, don't try to return fire, just duck. Understand?"

"Yes."

"In fact, here's what I want you to do," he said, changing his mind. "Go upstairs and pick out a window, and watch from there. If you have to fire, you'll have a better view from there. But don't fire unless I do."

"Wouldn't we be better off with you up there?" she asked.

Actually, they would. He could probably pick off one or two of the men from up there, but if they decided to simply bust down the front door, he didn't want to leave Kathy downstairs alone.

"You're worried about leaving me here alone," she said, reading his mind.

"I am," he agreed.

"Then why don't we just all go upstairs."

"If we hear them breaking in down here, we'd be too far away to do anything about it."

"But we'd be barricaded upstairs," she said.

Clint went to a narrow front window—there was one on either side of the main doors—and looked out. The four men with rifles were standing across the street, watching, waiting. Waiting for what? For their boss to make up his mind what to do?

From an upstairs window, he'd be able to pick them off if they started across the street. He might be able to keep them pinned down. But for how long?

"All right," he said. "Kathy, go upstairs and take Emily with you. Go to the front room that has the big desk and put her under it, or behind it. Sing out when you're there. Then you'll cover them while I come upstairs."

"Okay." She ran to the stairs, collected Emily from underneath them, and they both rushed up to the second floor.

"What are we waitin' for?" Chris asked.

"We don't want to go off half-cocked and get killed. According to Ned, the back door is barricaded, and so are the first-floor windows."

"Can't we just knock down the front door?" Billy asked.

"That's the Gunsmith in there, Billy," Steve said. "He's watching us from a window with a rifle in his hands. You want to start running for the doors?"

"No."

"Then shut up," Steve said. "We'll move when I say so."

"Do we wanna wait for the others?" Ned asked.

"We might want to," Steve said. "Right now I need somebody to cover the back. I don't want them sneaking out. Chris, that's you."

"By myself?"

"Again, do you wanna rush the front door?"

"No."

"Then cover the back. Anybody sticks their head out—*anybody*, and that includes the little girl—shoot it off."

"Yes, sir."

"And Chris, if you hear shooting, just stay where you are. Understand?"

"Yessir."

Chris trotted across the street and went down the alley to the rear of city hall.

"You really think he'd do it?" Ned asked. "Shoot the little girl?"

"I don't know," Steve said. "I don't really think Adams is gonna try to sneak out the back. He's more likely to call the four of us out into the street."

Billy's eyes went wide.

"Would you do that?"

"No," Steve said. "Even if we got him, he'd kill two, maybe three of us."

"So what do we do?" Ned asked.

"Well, first I want to pump lead into the building. Break the downstairs windows, and the upstairs windows, and fill the front doors with lead. Got me?"

"Yep," Ned said.

"Yessir," Billy said.

"Okay," Steve said, lifting his rifle, "now!"

They started firing.

"Okay!" Kathy shouted. "We're up here."

"Watch the window. I'm coming up!"

Clint ran up the steps. Halfway up, he heard the shooting start. Lead started shattering the windows and smacking into the front doors. He looked back. He had locked the front doors, and they were heavy oak, but he was thinking maybe he should have barricaded them, as well.

But when he heard the glass breaking upstairs, and Emily screaming, he continued up to the second floor.

THIRTY-THREE

When Clint reached the front room, Emily was crouched behind an overturned desk, holding her hands over her ears, and screaming.

Kathy was crouched below the window, shattered glass glinting in her hair.

Clint hit the floor and wrapped Emily in his arms. He stayed there until the shooting stopped.

"Kathy, you hit?"

"N-No."

"Emily, are you all right?"

"Make them stop, Clint."

"I'm going to try, baby. For now, you stay right behind this desk. Understand?"

"Y-Yes."

Clint stayed low and went to the window where Kathy was crouched. He peered out, saw three men across the street, reloading their rifles and their pistols.

"They'll probably do that one more time," he said. "We just have to stay low and wait it out. Emily, you go ahead and cover your ears, but you don't have to scream, okay? Nothing's going to hurt you."

"Okay."

And then the shooting started again. They all stayed low and waited for the men across the street to be empty. When it was over, Clint rose up, pointed his rifle, and fired . . .

Billy spun as the bullet struck him, and he hit the dirt. When Steve turned him over, he was dead.

"Damn!" he said. "Take cover."

He and Ned got behind a horse trough.

"Jesus," Ned said, "one shot and he got one of us."

"Maybe not the one he wanted," Steve said. "Or the one he should've killed."

"You? Because you're the boss?"

"Right."

"Well, he probably hit Billy 'cause he was the biggest target," Ned said.

"You're probably right."

"So what do we do now?"

"Stay behind cover, keep them pinned down and in until the others get here," Steve said. "When we have nine men, we'll be able to make a move."

Ned turned and pressed his shoulders against the horse trough.

"I'm hungry."

"Me, too," Steve said. "When the others get here, we can eat something."

"Well, they better get here damn quick," Ned said, "or I'll die of hunger."

Clint, Kathy, and Emily munched on some cold chicken while Clint kept an eye out the window. Kathy sat with Emily behind the desk, trying to keep the child's mind off what was happening.

He took a sip from his canteen. Kathy and Emily also had a canteen of water. He was going to have to check and see if there was a water supply inside the building.

The dead man remained in the street, where his friends

seemed content to leave him. The other two were hiding behind a horse trough. The fourth one was probably covering the back door. Briefly, Clint thought about going out the back on the two horses, but it would take time to get them through the doorway, and the flying lead might hit Emily. That was a plan that had "last resort" written all over it.

All the two men out front could do was pepper the building with lead from time to time, and wait. The boss, Steve, had probably gotten to the telegraph key before Clint destroyed it, and they were waiting for help to arrive.

Two more men?

More?

Probably more, if they were getting help to move all the loot. Clint figured five or six more, men who could load and drive a wagon and, probably, shoot.

Waiting was certainly in their favor. Maybe what he should do was step out and face the three men in the street, but would they go for that?

Well, he could ask.

"Kathy."

"Yes?"

"I want you to cover this window."

"What are you going to do?"

"I'm going down to the door to talk to these men."

"But . . . won't they shoot you as soon as you step out?" she asked.

"I won't step out," he told her. "I'll open the door enough to talk to them."

"What are you going to say?"

"I'm not sure," he said "I'll probably decide while I'm making my way down there. Come on, take my place."

She slid over after telling Emily to stay behind the desk and keep down.

Clint went to the door, then turned back to Kathy.

"Remember—"

"I know, I know," she said, "shoot anybody who sticks their head up."

"You've got it," he said.

He smiled at her.

"I'll be right back," he said.

"You better."

THIRTY-FOUR

Clint carefully open one of the doors a crack and called out, "You in the street? Steve?"

He waited.

"Jesus," Ned said, jumping as if he'd been struck by lightning, "he's callin' you by name."

"Come on, Ned," Steve said, "either you or Chris must've told him that much."

"Hey, but—"

"Never mind," Steve said. "Quiet. That you, Adams?" he called back.

Clint called out, "It's me. Can we talk?"

"Go ahead," Steve said. "Or better yet, why not step out and talk?"

"That's okay," Clint said. "I can hear you fine from here."

"Whatsamatter? Don't you trust me?"

"Afraid I don't know you well enough yet to do that," Clint responded.

"Okay, then," Steve said, "go ahead and talk."

"There are three of you and one of me," Clint said,

"but I'm still willing to step out and settle this in the street."

"I'll bet you are," Steve said, "but I think I can afford to wait awhile before we look at that as an option."

Clint fell silent after that. What else could he say?

"Anything else on your mind?" Steve asked.

"How about letting the woman and the child leave town?" Clint asked.

"Oh sure, send 'em out," Steve said, laughing. "We'll escort them to the city limit and see them on their way."

The sarcasm was thick in the man's tone. Once they got their hands on Emily, they'd used her as a hostage, so that was definitely out of the question.

"Afraid I've got nothing more to offer," Clint said.

"Suits me," Steve said.

Clint closed the door just as a hail of lead began to pepper it.

"Fire," Steve said, "and concentrate on those front doors."

"Gotcha!" Ned said.

Both men stood and began to fire. Lead started chewing pieces out of the wood. Steve knew none of the bullets were getting through, but it was just a message he was sending to the Gunsmith.

They began firing as quickly as they could lever fresh rounds into their rifles.

As the lead smacked ineffectually against the thick front doors, Clint made his way back upstairs. When he got there, Kathy was standing in front of the window, firing. She had broken the glass out of the windowpane so she could stick her rifle out.

Clint came up behind her, grabbed her, and pulled her down.

"But you told me to—" she said.

"I know what I told you," he said, "but save your ammunition. They're just trying to make a statement."

"So that didn't go really well, did it?" she asked after the firing had stopped.

"No," Clint said, "but then I didn't think they'd go for it."

"Do you have another plan?"

"Sort of," he said.

"Care to share?"

"Well, they sent the young kid—Chris—to cover the back. As far as I'm concerned, that's their weak link."

"How do we take advantage of it?"

"Well, I'm considering a couple of things," Clint said. "I'll tell you when I've made up my mind."

"All right."

"You can go back and sit with Emily for a while," he said. "I'll take it from here."

"Okay."

Clint risked a look out the window. The two men had stopped firing and were once again crouched behind the horse trough. Clint settled down to watch and try to come up with a plan.

Behind the trough, Steve and Ned reloaded their rifles.

"He thinks he can take the three of us," Ned said.

"And maybe he can," Steve said.

"I thought you were fast."

"I am," Steve said, "but that don't mean I want to test myself against the Gunsmith. I'm lookin' to face him in a situation I can control. That means havin' seven men behind me, not two."

"Well," Ned said, "can't say I blame ya for that. So what do we do now?"

"We wait."

"You want me to spell Chris in the back?"

"No," Steve said, "leave the kid there. I need you right here in front."

"All we're doin' is makin' a mess outta the front of city hall," Ned said.

"We're doin' more than that," Steve said.

"Like what?"

"We're givin' them something to think about," Steve explained. "That's what."

THIRTY-FIVE

As it turned out, Clint waited too long.

Steve Harwick waited just long enough.

Steve heard the sounds of wagons, looked up the street, and saw the wagons coming down toward him. Three buckboards, and three more mounted men.

"Hey," Ned said, "they got here quick, and early."

"Good," Steve said. "We can use them."

"We gonna charge the building now?" Ned asked.

"Not yet."

"Then what?"

"You and a few of the boys are gonna keep Adams pinned down, while I get the others to start packing up our loot. Once we have things packed and ready to go, we'll take care of Adams." "What if he makes a move?"

"As soon as we hear the shootin', we'll come runnin'," Steve said. "We can even put another man in the back with Chris. Two front, two back, the rest busy packin'."

"What if we just pack up and leave?" Ned asked. "You think he'd come after us?"

"No, but he'd talk to the law about us. Or the woman would. And if there's anythin' illegal about what we're doin', then the law would be after us."

"Why not talk to the doc and find out?"

"He put me in charge of this operation," Steve said. "I'm not gonna bother Brock until I have what he sent us here to get. He went to a lot of trouble to set this up. I'm not gonna be the one to ruin it."

As the wagons approached them, Steve stood up and waved them on, then followed them. He collared one horseman and instructed him to stay with Ned.

"He'll explain the situation to you," he said.

The man nodded, and dismounted, letting Steve have his horse. He rode to the front of the three wagons and showed them the way to the stockyards.

"What's going on?" Kathy asked.

"Looks like the Calvary has arrived," he said.

"For us?" she asked, excited.

"No, no," he said, "for them. Their extra men just got here, riding down the street in their wagons."

"How many?"

"Three wagons, but six men," Clint said.

"So that's it, then," she said mournfully, "we're as good as finished."

"Not yet we aren't," he said.

"What are you thinking?"

"I'm thinking about the roof."

"You said we didn't have to worry about the roof," she said. "That the building was too high."

"It's higher than the buildings on either side," he admitted, "but maybe we can get to a roof from a second- or third-floor window."

"But wouldn't that be dangerous?" she asked. "Especially for Emily?"

"We'll have to see," Clint said. "It looks like they're going to leave us alone for a while so they can fill the new men in on what's going on."

"So what do we do?"

"We change places again," Clint said. "You watch the window while I check the rooftops outside the windows."

While she skittered across the floor to the window, Emily asked him, "Can I come with you?"

He started to say no, but then decided nobody was going to be shooting at him.

"Okay," he said, "but you have to do exactly what I tell you to do."

"I will," she promised.

"Okay, then let's go." He looked at Kathy, who was peering above the windowsill. "We'll be right back."

"And I'll be right here," she promised.

THIRTY-SIX

The roof of the building on the right side of city hall was fairly even with the windows of the second floor. The rooftop of the building to the left was a few steps down from the third floor. Clint thought he could easily open the window and drop down. The question was: Could Kathy and Emily make it?

There was an alley alongside the buildings—well, not exactly an alley, but there was some separation between the buildings—but Clint felt sure he could make the jump. If Kathy could make it, he thought he could toss Emily across. But could Kathy catch her? Or if they switched places, could Emily toss her while he was the one to catch her?

Or could he make the jump with Emily on his back?

"What are you lookin' at?" Emily asked.

"The roof next door," he said.

She moved to the window and looked.

"Are we goin' there?"

"Why? Do you think you could jump over there?"

She looked again, then looked back at him as if he was crazy.

"No," she said, shaking her head.

"Well then," he said, "let's go back to Kathy . . ."

* * *

Steve got the men started on loading the wagons.

"Get this done and then we got some other business to tend to," he told them.

"Like what?" Joe Seymour asked.

"Clint Adams."

"The Gunsmith?" Seymour asked. "What's he got to do with anythin'?"

"He's here, that's what," Steve said. "And he's tryin' to stop us."

"Why is it his business?"

"I don't know," Steve said. "He's makin' it his business."

"Why don't he just leave town." Then Seymour got it. "Wait. He thinks he's sick?"

"He might think he's infected, yeah," Steve said.

"Then he's a sucker, like everybody else," Seymour said.

"That may be," Steve said, "but it don't really matter. Sick or not, he's gonna be dead."

"The Gunsmith, huh?" Seymour asked as the other men were loading the wagon. "You think we got enough men?"

"We've got nine. Should be enough."

"Nine? But you had five already."

"He killed two."

Seymour frowned.

"Maybe we should send for more," he suggested.

"Can't. He disabled the telegraph key. We're gonna have to make do with nine."

"Where is he now?"

"We've got him pinned down in city hall, along with a woman and a little girl."

"He's at a disadvantage if he's got to look out for them," Seymour said.

"Exactly. Now let's get these wagons loaded so we can take care of him."

"I'll hurry the men up," Seymour promised.

"And then meet me across from city hall."

"Gotcha."

"What are they doing?" Kathy asked.

"They're waiting," Clint said.

"For what?"

"If I had to guess, I'd say they're loading up their loot and saving me—us—for later. They figure they've got us pinned down real good."

"Don't they?"

"Well . . . maybe not."

"What do you mean?"

"I have an idea, but it's risky."

"Tell me."

He told her.

Steve came back to city hall, joined Ned and the other man—Philips—behind the horse trough.

"You fill him in?" Steve asked Ned.

"I did, yeah."

"Philips, I want you to go around back. You'll find a young guy named Chris there. You watch the back with him."

"Right." Philips preferred his job to what the others were doing, loading up the wagons, so he had no complaint.

"And what do we do?" Ned asked.

"Just relax," Steve said. "When the others have finished loading everythin', they'll join us here and then we'll go in and get him."

"And then we can quit this town?"

"That's right."

"Good," Ned said, "it gives me the willies."

"You're not believin' that story about an epidemic, are you?" Steve asked.

"I'm just sayin'," Ned replied, "an empty town with only some dead bodies in it—that would spook anybody."

"You can't get spooked by a few dead bodies, Ned," Steve told him.

"Maybe *you* can't . . ." Ned said.

"What do you mean 'throw her'?" Kathy asked, lowering her voice.

"Well, there's a little gap we'd have to get over," Clint said.

"A gap? Like an alley?"

"Not an alley," Clint said. "Not that wide."

"So which one of us would catch and which one would throw?" she asked.

"That's what I'm thinking about," Clint said. "Why don't you go up and have a look, then come back and tell me."

"I'll have a look," Kathy said, "but this doesn't sound too good to me."

Kathy went upstairs into the room Clint had described and looked out the window at the rooftop he was talking about. Her eyes went wide. She knew it wasn't ten feet away, but it might as well have been. She looked down. If somebody fell into that space . . .

She stopped thinking about jumping and considered the prospect of tossing Emily across. That just made her shudder. She could just see the child's body plummeting to the ground.

It was risky, but if they remained where they were, they were very likely going to be killed. And she didn't have any better ideas to offer.

She turned and went back down to the second floor to rejoin Clint and Emily.

"Well?" Clint asked when Kathy came back in.

She shrugged and said, "Let's do it."

THIRTY-SEVEN

"They still in that window?" Steve asked.

"Last I saw," Ned said, "the woman was stickin' her head up."

"Let's send some lead in there, just to remind them we're out here."

"Okay."

They raised their rifles and started firing.

There was no glass left in the window to shatter, but the bullets slammed into the window frame, breaking it apart, and into the wall and ceiling beyond.

But nobody was in the room to notice.

Clint sent Kathy and Emily up to the third floor while he ran downstairs, then followed them up and into the room where he'd chosen to go out the window.

"What do you want to do?" he asked Kathy. "Toss or catch?"

"I think I better catch," she said. "I don't trust myself to throw her that far."

"Throw who?" Emily asked, her eyes wide.

"I'll explain," Clint said, crouching down in front of her.

"The only way we have to get out of this building is to jump to the next roof."

Emily bit her lip. She walked to the window, looked out, looked down, then turned to look at Clint.

"Okay," she said.

"That should do it," Steve said, reloading his rifle. "If that doesn't keep their heads down for a while, nothin' will."

"So now we just watch?" Ned asked.

"And wait," Steve said.

Clint opened the window.

"All right," he told Kathy.

"You're going to have to help me," she said.

"I will. Come on, hold on to my hands. I'll lower you down."

She had to lift her dress to climb out the window, exposing her legs and thighs. He found it oddly erotic at that moment. He took her hands and lowered her out the window.

"I can't jump," she said, looking down. "I'm frightened. You'll have to swing me."

"I can't swing you," he said. "You're flat against the wall, I can't get you swinging. Wait, I have an idea."

"Good," she said.

"Put your feet against the wall," he said. "When I say go, I'll let go and you push off. You'll land on the roof."

"Are you sure?"

"I'm positive," he lied.

"Be careful, Kathy," Emily said.

"It's a little too late for that," Kathy said.

"Come on," Clint said, "put your feet flat against the wall."

"A-All right. There."

"Okay. I'll count to three, and let go. On three, you push off. Got it?"

"On three," she said. "Got it."

"Okay," he said, "one . . . two . . . three . . ."

He let go.

She pushed off.

She flew through the air, and for a moment she thought that she would surely plummet to the ground—and then she landed on the roof with a bone-jarring thud.

"Ooh!"

For a moment everything froze, and then she said, "I made it!"

"Shhh, not so loud," he said. "They have somebody in the back. Okay, now you have to catch Emily."

"All right. Wait." She got up, rubbed her ass, which had absorbed the brunt of the landing. "All right, I'm ready."

Clint lifted Emily and said, "Don't worry."

"I'm not worried," the little girl said. "You won't let me fall."

Clint carried Emily to the window and leaned out with her.

"Are you ready?" he asked Kathy.

Kathy took a deep breath and said, "I'm ready."

"I'm going to count," Clint said, "one, two, three, and then toss her. Ready?"

Kathy braced her legs and said, "Ready," thinking, This is crazy.

"Are you ready?" Clint asked Emily.

"I'm ready," she said, and kissed him on the cheek.

"One . . . two . . . three . . ."

He tossed Emily over to the roof. She flew through the air, her arms waving, and right into Kathy's arms. The woman caught her, and then fell on her ass again on the roof.

"Oooh!" she said again.

"You caught me!" Emily said happily. "Can we do that again?"

Clint climbed onto the windowsill, leaned out, and just

before he jumped, he thought about the horses, which were still in the building. He was going to have to make sure he got Eclipse back.

He jumped.

"When are they gonna get here?" Ned asked.

"Relax," Steve said, "it'll take them a while to load the wagons."

"What do we do then? Just charge the door?"

"No," Steve said, "I have a plan."

"What is it?"

"I'll tell you when the others come," Steve said. "Be patient."

"I been patient," Ned complained. "I want out of this town."

"Soon," Steve said, "very soon . . ."

Clint hit the roof with the soles of his feet, his knees bent. The impact wasn't too bad.

"You made it!" Emily said, clapping her hands.

"We all made it," he said. "Are you both all right?"

"I'm fine," Kathy said. "I'll be a little sore, but fine."

"I'm okay," Emily said, "but what about Eclipse?"

"I'll get Eclipse back," Clint said, "as soon as I get the two of you someplace safe."

"Where?" Kathy asked.

"I don't know," Clint said. "Let's get off this roof and find a place."

They found a hatch that would let them into the building, which turned out to be a dress shop with living quarters on the second floor.

They made their way down to the main floor and Clint led them behind the counter.

"Wait here," he said. "I'll look out the window."

He walked to the front window and peered out. He could see the men across the street. It was obvious they would not be able to go out the front door without being seen.

"Stay there," he said again. "I'll check the back."

He went through the shop to the storeroom, found the back door, and opened it a crack. He could see that there were two men behind city hall, watching the back door. He doubted they could sneak out that way.

Had he traded one prison for another, at the same time putting the horses out of their reach?

THIRTY-EIGHT

Clint found his way back to the store and crouched behind the counter with Kathy and Emily.

"Well?" Kathy asked.

"We can't get out the front," he said. "They'll see us. And there are two men in the back."

"So what do we do?"

"I may have to step out the back and take care of those two, but they'll hear the shots out front. We'd have to make a run for it."

"We could do that," she said, "but can't we climb out a first-floor window? That'd be easier than what we just did."

"We could," Clint said, "but there are no windows on either side. We'll have to go out the back."

"And kill those men."

"Yes."

"And then run."

"Yes," he said, "but where to? We don't want to get caught out in the open. You two know the town better than I do."

"Well," Kathy said, "there are a lot of places in this part of town that we can hide."

"Good," Clint said, "that's what the two of you are going to do. Run and hide."

"What about you?"

"I'm going the other way," he said. "We need those horses, and maybe I can get rid of a few more men."

"But . . . there are so many of them."

"That's why we've got to get rid of some," Clint said. "I need to get the odds more in my favor."

"Well, I'll tell you where we're going to hide—"

"No," he said, "Don't. Just in case something goes wrong, I don't want to know."

"You're afraid if they catch you, they'll make you tell."

"I don't think they could make me tell," he said, "but you never know. So it's better if I really don't know."

"You're going to get killed," Kathy said, raising her voice.

"I don't want you to get killed!" Emily shouted.

"Shhh," Clint said, "keep your voices down. I'm not going to get killed, Emily. I'm going to get Eclipse, and the other horse, and we're leaving town."

"What about your being sick?"

"If I haven't gotten sick by now, I'm probably okay," he reasoned. "At least, I hope so."

"Okay, so when do we do this?"

"Well," he said, "now is as good a time as any."

Several men came walking up the street toward Steve and Ned, led by Joe Seymour.

"What's goin' on?" Steve asked. "Finished already?"

"Almost done," Seymour said, "I left a couple of the boys there to wrap everything up."

Seymour had two men with him, and they had two in the back. That made seven. Seven against one—the one being the Gunsmith.

"Maybe," he said, "we'll wait for the other two—" He stopped when he heard the shots.

* * *

Clint said, "When I open the door and step out, you come out behind me and start running. Don't stop, and don't turn around to look."

"Okay."

"Emily? You keep running, you hear?"

"I hear."

"Okay."

Clint walked to the back door and took a breath. He opened it and stepped out.

"Go!" he hissed.

They came out behind him and started to run.

One of the two men behind city hall saw them and yelled, "Hey!"

The other men looked, and they both went for their guns.

Clint drew and fired twice.

"What the hell—" Ned said.

"Behind the building," Steve said. "Let's go!"

THIRTY-NINE

Clint froze as the two men fell.

The others would be coming up the alley, so he couldn't go that way. And if he turned to run after Kathy and Emily, they might spot him and follow. He wanted to keep them well away from the girls.

His only option was that small space between city hall and the dress shop, not exactly an alley. In fact, barely wide enough for him to get through. If they caught him in there, he'd be a sitting duck.

If they looked there.

He ran to the narrow opening and had to turn sideways to fit. He holstered his gun and slid in, began making his way along toward the front, hoping to get there before anyone looked for him in that tight space.

Steve ran up the alley with Ned, Joe Seymour, and the others behind him. They stopped when they saw the two dead men behind the building.

"Check that back door!" Steve said.

Ned ran over and tried it.

"Locked! How'd they get out?"

"Maybe Adams got out, but the other two might still be

inside," Steve said. "Check down there." He pointed the way Kathy and Emily had run, already well out of sight.

Seymour and one of the other men ran that way, while Steve joined Ned at the door. The other man checked the bodies to make sure they were dead.

"They dead?" Steve asked.

"Yup," the man said, "one shot each."

Steve tried the door again. It moved, then stopped.

"It's not locked," he said. "It's blocked. The two of you, put your shoulders to it. Get it open."

Ned and the other man obeyed. They slammed their shoulders into the door until wood splintered and the door opened.

Steve stepped inside, saw the shattered piece of furniture that had been blocking it.

"All right," he said, "search the building."

Ned and the other man went inside while Steve waited where he was. Just in case Adams was inside, he didn't want to walk into a bullet. He also wanted to wait for Seymour and the other man to come back.

That was when he noticed the gap between city hall and the building to its right.

Clint kept moving as quickly as he could, but it seemed to him like he was crawling. He was actually shuffling his feet, alternately scraping his back and front against the walls.

And he'd made a mistake. He had holstered his gun, and then slid between the buildings with his right side first. If someone spotted him, he would be hard pressed to get his gun out and pointed back there. He'd trapped himself into an untenable position, if he was caught.

He continued to shuffle as quickly as he could.

Steve frowned. It wasn't an alley, really, just a space between buildings. He assumed it went all the way through, though.

* * *

Would Adams be dumb enough to get himself trapped in there?

He left the doorway and walked over to have a look.

Clint reached the front of the buildings, stepped out into the street, and quickly looked back. He saw a shadow and ducked out of the way. At the same time he looked around to see if any of the men had been left in front. There was no one.

He ran for the front door of city hall. Before going up with Kathy and Emily, he'd run down and unlocked the front doors. Now he opened them and stepped back into city hall. He immediately went to the courtroom, where he'd stashed both Eclipse and the other horse. He had to get them outside where he could run with them.

Steve peered into the slim aperture between the buildings, was able to see all the way through to the front. There was nobody in the way. He turned as he heard two men running back to him.

"Didn't see nobody," Seymour said.

"Did you check some of the buildings?"

"Yeah. Some were locked, others weren't. We went inside, and looked in windows, but didn't see anybody."

"Can either one of you track?"

Both men just stared at him.

"Never mind. Get inside and help Ned search the building."

"Right," Seymour said. The two men entered the building.

"Check downstairs," Ned told the man with him. They had gone up the back stairs to the second floor, Ned wanting to check the window Adams and the woman had been using.

The other man—Rafe—nodded, and headed for the front steps.

As Clint came out of the courtroom with Eclipse and the other horse, Rafe appeared on the stairway. The two men stared at each other for a split second, and then Rafe made a panicked grab for his gun. Clint drew and cleanly shot the man in the chest. As the man tumbled down the steps, Clint quickly walked the two horses out the front doorway.

FORTY

Ned heard the shot from the room upstairs.

Seymour and the man with him—Dylan—heard the shot before they started up the back stairs. They reversed their direction and rushed to the front hall. Rafe had come to a stop at the bottom of the steps.

"He's dead," Seymour said, looking at the open front doors. "Dylan, check outside."

Dylan hesitated.

"I ain't stickin' my head out there," he said. "That's the Gunsmith. What if he's waitin'?"

"He's probably runnin'," Seymour said. "Go ahead and look!"

Dylan moved slowly to the front door then reluctantly stuck his head out. He heaved a sigh when he saw nothing.

"Nobody there!" he said as Steve Harwick came running into the hall.

"What happened?" He looked down at Rafe. Ned appeared at the top of the steps at that point.

"There's an open window up here," he said. "Looks like they jumped onto the roof next door."

Steve closed his eyes. He'd discounted the roof, since city

hall was the tallest building in town. It didn't occur to him they'd go out a window above the first floor.

Damn it!

Clint quickly mounted Eclipse when he got outside, and led the other horse around the first corner and out of sight. He hoped he was going the right way. Considering the direction Kathy and Emily had run, he hoped they were hiding in one of these empty buildings, and would be able to see him riding in the street.

If they were inside and hiding under a desk or a counter, they wouldn't see him at all—and he dared not call out.

And he couldn't ride out in the open for very long. Steve or one of his men might spot him. His eyes kept scanning the storefronts, hoping to spot them looking out the window, so when Emily ran out at him from his left when he was looking right, he was surprised.

"Clint!" She reached him and hung on to his leg. "You're not shot!"

"No, I'm not." He reached down for her and lifted her up into the saddle in front of him, not behind. He wanted to be able to shield her if lead started flying, not the other way around.

Kathy came trotting out of the same store and said, "You're safe."

"Yes," he said. "Get mounted, quickly."

She lifted her skirts and quickly scrambled into the saddle of the other horse.

"Now let's get out of here," he said.

They rode out of town, leaving the disease and the killers behind, but they went barely a couple of miles when Kathy reined her horse in.

"Wait," she said.

"What's wrong?"

"We can't do this," she said.

"Why not?"

"We're leaving them alone to loot the entire town at will," she said.

"What can we do?" he asked. "Or rather what can I do, because that's what you mean, right? That I can't do this?"

"If it wasn't for us," she said, "if you weren't trying to keep us safe, wouldn't you try to stop them?"

"No," he said. "There's too many of them, and the town has been abandoned."

"I don't believe you," she said. "How many of them have you killed already?"

"Three or four."

"Four," she said. "There are seven left."

"See, that's what I mean," he told her. "I'm pretty badly outnumbered."

"But you have an advantage."

"Explain that to me."

"They don't know where you are," she said. "They might even been thinking that you left town."

"I did," Clint said. "They're probably already driving out of town with their loot."

"Then you can track them," she said, "see where they go, and then turn them over to the law."

He remained silent, because he hated to admit that made any sense.

"And maybe you can find where the rest of the townspeople went," she added. "Including Emily's parents."

"And what are you going to do?"

"Emily and I will ride to the nearest town, just as you planned. What did you say the name was?"

"Givens."

"Right. And when we get there, I'll talk to the law. I'll get them to send out some help for you."

Clint hesitated.

"Let me have Emily," she said, bringing her horse closer to his. "And I have my rifle. I'll take care of her."

Reluctantly, he lifted Emily and handed her over to Kathy, who settled the girl in front of her.

"Are you gonna find my mommy and daddy, Clint?" she asked, looking at him with big, wide eyes.

Damn it, that just wasn't fair, he thought. With that look on her face, how could he tell her no?

"I guess I am, little one."

FORTY-ONE

"Should we keep lookin' for him?" Ned asked Steve.

"Let's get everything loaded up, and I'll think about it," Steve told him.

They left the dead men where they lay and returned to the stockyards. The loot was almost all loaded up. Two of the buckboards had been covered with a tied-down tarp, and the other two were almost ready.

"We got everything on four wagons?" Steve asked.

"That happens when you know how to load a wagon," one of the men said proudly.

"Hey," the other man said, "where are—"

"Dead," Steve said, cutting him off. "You wanna complain about getting a bigger cut?"

"Not me," the man said.

Steve said to Ned, "Help them get that last wagon tied down."

"Yeah, okay."

While they loaded the last wagon, Steve gave the situation some thought. Now that they had let Adams get out of city hall with the woman and the child, they could have been anywhere. To start searching the town again would be a fruitless waste of time.

No, as soon as they had things ready, they were getting out. Let Adams have the abandoned town for as long as he wanted, and let Brock handle the fallout.

Stuart Brock was killing time waiting for his men to arrive with the loot by sampling the whores that the town of Givens had to offer.

One of the whores had said to him, "Ain't it odd that a doctor likes whores? Ain't you worried about diseases?"

That had earned her a slap across the face, after which he'd had her thrown out by Hale without paying her.

This whore had apparently learned from the others. She hardly spoke, and went about her business with a certain amount of enthusiasm.

She was long and lean, with flat breasts but lovely nipples, which suited him. She was crouched over him now, sucking his stiff penis, going at it like a mule to a salt lick. It was lucky for her that she had spoken to all the other girls who had been with Brock, so that she pretty much knew what he liked.

She sucked him noisily, which Amanda had told her he liked, and made sounds like "mmm," and "ummmm," which she had learned from Denise, who apparently had not made enough noise.

And when he abruptly flipped her onto her back and bulled his way into her, she gasped (thanks, Betty), wrapped her legs around his waist (Samantha), and urged him to fuck her harder (thanks to Georgia).

She thought she was doing pretty good, and had to admit that the man had a lot of stamina, which suited her just fine. She was one of the older whores, but rather than being tired of the business, she still enjoyed a good fucking.

Daniel Hale stood outside his boss's door and listened to him go at it with the old whore. Hale was the one who had

to bring the girls to Brock, and there were a few he'd preferred to this one—usually younger and with more in the
way of meat on their bones. But he knew his boss was particular about his whores. Hell, he was particular about everything. Except maybe the men he hired.

Hale never liked Steve Harwick, and didn't agree with
Brock's decision to let the man head up the Medicine Bow
job. But there was no way he could have ever told Brock
that. Not without losing his job for questioning the man.

So he just stood and waited for the man to finish and call
for him. He might be called upon to escort the woman from
the property—with or without pay—or to take some time
off, meaning Brock would be keeping the woman with him
for a while. In that case he'd go out onto the porch to wait
and watch for Harwick and the others.

But that was what Daniel Hale did best—watch and wait.

"Are we ready?" Steve Harwick asked.

Ned looked behind them at the four wagons, and the
mounted men. They had some extra horses thanks to the
men Clint Adams had killed, and they were simply tied to
the last wagon, like a remuda.

"All right," Steve said. "Let's go. We're done here."

Clint watched as the column of four wagons and seven men
left Medicine Bow. He had two choices. Hit-and-run—that
is, kill one or two, run for it, then follow them again, and
hit them again. Or he could simply follow them to where
they were going and find out who they were working for—
because he doubted this fellow Steve was the mastermind
behind this.

He followed along behind them, running the whole thing
over in his mind. Who would have planned such a thing, to
take advantage of an epidemic disease in order to rape a
whole town?

* * *

"It's gonna take us two days," Steve said to Ned. "I want you to ride on ahead and tell the boss we're comin'. You'll be able to make it by tonight."

"I can do that," Ned said, "but what about Adams?"

"Adams is still hidin' out with the woman and the child," Steve said. "And even if he does come after us, there are six of us. Out in the open, he won't have a chance."

"I hope not," Ned said.

"Just ride on ahead," Steve said. "Tell Dr. Brock we're comin'."

"Okay," Ned said. "You're the boss."

"Right," Steve said. "I am."

As Ned rode off, Seymour rode up alongside Steve and asked, "Where's he off to?"

"To let Brock know we're coming."

"You know, that's the one thing I can't figure in all this," Seymour said.

"What's that?"

"A doctor plannin' the whole thing," Seymour said. "Ain't they supposed to be . . . well, good?"

"Doctors are men, too," Steve said. "This one decided to make himself some money."

"How much you think all this stuff is worth?" Seymour asked.

"I think it's all worth somethin' because there's so much of it," Steve said. "We did find some cash—a lot of cash, as a matter of fact—and some good furniture. All in all, it's a good haul."

"You ever done one like this before?" Seymour asked. "A job like this, I mean? Takin' a whole town?"

"Never before," Steve said, "but then I never threw in with a doctor before. A doctor with a plan."

"Well," Seymour said, "thanks for bringin' me in on it, Steve."

"I needed men I could count on, Joe."

Seymour nodded, dropped back to ride alongside one of the wagons.

Clint saw Ned ride on ahead of the column and made the immediate decision to follow him. The only reason he could see for Ned to ride ahead would be to tell someone—report to someone—that the rest of them were on their way. That meant Ned was on his way to talk to the boss. However, if Clint was wrong, if Ned was simply riding to the next town to have a drink in a saloon, Clint could confront him and make him talk. He'd know who planned the robbery of a whole town, and where the townspeople all went.

And find Emily's parents.

FORTY-TWO

Clint followed Ned from well behind. There was no chance the man would notice him. But Ned never even turned in his saddle. He was apparently unconcerned about the possibility of being followed. He would lead Clint right to the man who'd planned the job.

Ned rode right up to the main house of the Bar Double-B Ranch. He dismounted and handed the reins of his horse to a man who knew him.

"Hey, Ned."

"Sam. Boss in?"

"You'll have to talk to Hale first."

"Oh yeah, Hale," Ned said. "He's still here?"

"They served together in the war," Sam said. "Hale was Brock's aide. That makes men form a bond."

"Yeah, right," Ned said. He had never formed any sort of bond with another man, so he didn't understand. "There'll be men and wagons here tomorrow," he told Sam. "Better get ready to take care of them."

"Okay."

Ned went up the steps to the front door and knocked.

* * *

Clint watched from a high knoll as the two men talked, and
then Ned went to the front door. The ranch seemed sparsely
populated at the moment. Either the ranch hands were away,
or it wasn't a working ranch. There were no horses in the
corral. There was plenty of room for the wagons and horses,
not to mention the loot. Perhaps that was why there were no
men. They had been sent to Medicine Bow.

The lone man he did see walked Ned's horse to the livery.
Clint decided there were no other men around. And the one
who was there wouldn't know him when he rode in.

He mounted Eclipse and started down to the house.

Hale opened the door and looked at Ned.

"What are you doing here?"

"Reporting in," Ned said. "Harwick sent me on ahead."

"Is it done?"

"It's done."

"All right," Hale said. "Come on in."

Ned entered and Hale closed the door behind him, then
turned to face Ned.

"Follow me," Hale said.

Ned knew the way, but he followed Hale anyway. The
man was only doing his job.

Clint rode up to the house, alert for the appearance of the
man in the barn. When he came out and saw Clint, he
walked over to him. Clint waited, not dismounting. He was
hoping to talk his way into the house without gunplay. The
man approaching him was wearing a gun on his hip, so Clint
would have to be careful.

"Help ya?"

"I want to see your boss."

"Dr. Brock?"

Helpful.

"Yes, Dr. Brock."

"I don't think he sees anybody without an appointment."

"Tell him it's an emergency," Clint said. "Tell him I may be carrying a plague."

"What?" The man took several steps back.

"Just tell him."

"Yeah, okay," the man said, putting even more distance between them. "You wait here."

Clint nodded, still did not dismount. He wanted to be ready to move fast, if he had to. Evasive action would be better on horseback.

"What are you doing?" Hale demanded as Sam came down the hall toward Brock's office. Ned was inside with the boss.

"Somebody at the door," Sam said. "There's a fella outside wants to see the doc."

"What for?"

"He says he might be carrying a plague."

"What?"

"That's what he said."

"What's his name?"

"Um, I don't know."

"Did you ask?"

"No."

Hale shook his head and said, "Wait here." He knocked and went inside.

Dr. Stuart Brock looked away from Ned, who was sitting in front of him, to focus on Hale as he entered.

"Yes, Hale?"

"There's a man outside, boss, wants to see you."

"Me?" Brock asked. "Or a doctor?"

"You," Hale said, even though he wasn't sure it was the right answer.

Brock looked at Ned.

"Were you followed?"

"I don't think so."

Brock gave him a hard stare. "Yes or no?"

"No."

"It could be Clint Adams," Brock said to Hale.

"The Gunsmith?"

"Yes," Brock said. "These idiots allowed him to get involved in our operation."

"So what do we do?" Hale asked.

"Get your gun," Brock said. "Take Ned with you, let him have a look out the window. If it's Adams, let him in and bring him here."

"Then what?"

"Then you and Ned stand outside that door. Got it?"

"Got it, boss."

Brock looked at Ned. "Go!"

"Sure thing."

Ned got up and followed Hale out. Brock opened his right-hand drawer, took out a Colt, checked to make sure it was loaded, and then put it back.

He sat back to await his guest.

FORTY-THREE

Clint kept his eyes on the front of the house. Briefly, he thought he saw somebody at one of the front windows. A few moments later the front door opened and a man stepped out. He was short, about five-eight, stocky, in his forties, wearing a black suit.

"Are you waiting to see the doctor?" he asked.

"That's right."

"Come this way, then," the man said. "You can leave your horse there. No one will touch it."

Clint knew that Eclipse wouldn't allow anyone to touch him. He dismounted and ascended the steps.

"My name is Hale," the man said, not offering a hand. "Come this way."

He entered the house and Clint went in behind him. There was no one else there. He waited while Hale closed the door.

"What's your name?" Hale asked.

"Clint Adams."

"I know that name," the man said. "It's very famous."

"Kind of."

"Come with me."

He did not take Clint to Dr. Brock's office, where he had left his boss. Instead, he took him to an examination room farther back in the house, where Brock was waiting. He was wearing his white doctor's jacket, and had a stethoscope around his neck.

"Hello," the doctor said. He was a tall, slender man about Hale's age. "I'm Dr. Brock."

"Hello."

"Please, sit. What seems to be the trouble?" Brock asked. He moved around behind his desk and sat. Clint remained standing. "You said something to Sam about a plague?"

"Plague, disease," Clint said, shrugging his shoulders. "I don't know what it was, but I've been exposed to it. I thought I should see a doctor."

"That's all right, Mr. Hale," Brock said. "You can wait right outside."

"Yes, Doctor."

Hale left, closing the door behind him.

"Why don't you start by telling me where you think you contracted this disease?" Brock asked.

"I think you already know."

"Do I?"

"I recognize your name from papers in your office in Medicine Bow, Doctor," Clint said. "I know you were their doctor."

"That's no secret."

"Tell me about the epidemic."

"It came on suddenly," Brock said. "People began to die. There was nothing I could do."

"So you left with the others?"

"That's right."

"And left the sick behind, unattended? Like the little girl, Emily? And a woman named Kathy?"

"Did they survive?"

"They did."

"I'm glad."

"Sure you are," Clint said. "Tell me, where did the towns-people go? Where did Emily's parents go?"

"They headed for Flint," Brock said. "I don't know if the people there will let them in, though."

"And you don't care," Clint said, "because you came here and put your plan into motion to rape the town."

"Rape?" Brock asked. "I prefer to think of it as . . . recovering."

"And selling?"

Brock spread his arms. "Well, I can hardly keep it all for myself."

"You could return it."

"Why would I bother taking it if I was going to return it?" Brock asked.

"Tell me something," Clint said. "Why haven't I contracted this disease?"

"You must have a natural immunity," the doctor said, "as did the girl and Kathy."

"But they were sick."

"If they came through it, they're immune."

"Well, they did, and they are probably already in Givens, talking to the law."

"That's not a problem since you're the only one who knows I'm involved."

"I'll talk to the sheriff in Flint when I get there."

"When, or if?" Brock asked, his hand inching toward his desk drawer.

"Go ahead and go for that gun in your drawer," Clint said.

Brock pulled his hand away as if burned, then smiled.

"I wouldn't dare draw on the Gunsmith," he said, "but there are two men with guns outside that door."

"If they come in, you're the first one I'll shoot."

That didn't sit well with Brock. He recognized that he had made the wrong play. His eyes went to the drawer that contained the gun.

"You're a doctor first, not a crook, Brock," Clint said. "You've misplayed this whole matter. What makes you think Steve Harwick is even bringing the loot here?"

"What—he sent Ned ahead to say he was coming."

"And you believed him?"

"I have the connections to sell everything."

"I think Harwick could handle that himself."

"You're wrong."

"We could wait and see," Clint said, "but first I'll take that gun. Open the drawer . . . slowly."

FORTY-FOUR

Clint could tell Brock's mind was working. Was he right about Harwick? Could the doctor reach his gun in time?

"Feel free to try," Clint said. "Open it. I'll give you a chance."

"No," Brock said, "as you said, I'm a doctor, not a gunman."

"Call your men in," Clint said.

"They'll come in shooting."

"For your sake, I hope not."

"Hale? Ned? Come in here."

The door opened and the two men came rushing in, their guns out. At the same time Brock went for the gun in his drawer.

Clint moved swiftly. He drew his gun with his right hand, at the same time stepping to the desk and slamming the drawer on Brock's hand. He fired, killing both Hale and Ned before they had a chance to pull the triggers of their weapons. Then he removed the gun from the top drawer.

Brock sat back in his chair, cradling his injured hand.

"Now," Clint said, "we'll wait and see if Harwick appears with your loot. Personally, I hope he does."

"And when he does, he and his men will kill you."

"They'll try."

"Who else is in the house?"

"Only the cook."

"And your other men?"

"Just Sam. The rest are with Harwick," Brock said. "This is not a working ranch, so I have no hands."

That confirmed what Clint had surmised.

"All right," he said, "we'll have the cook prepare some food and you can tell me your plan for all your profits. Perhaps to set up a new practice?"

"No more town doctor's office for me," Brock said. "I have bigger plans."

"Tell me over supper."

They ate a fine supper prepared by Brock's cook, who clearly hated her boss. Clint could tell by the way she looked at the doctor. And she smirked afterward when Clint tied the man to his chair for the night.

"You're going to make me sleep like this?" he demanded.

"I don't care if you sleep or not," Clint said. "Just that you don't move while I sleep."

"I'll keep watch if you like," the woman said. She was a middle-aged woman with gray hair, but lively blue eyes.

"Where do you live?" he asked.

"Here," she said. "He makes me live here."

"Are you married?"

"Yes, I have a husband in Flint."

"How far is it?"

"A few hours."

"Then take a horse in the morning and go home."

"I can go now," she said. "I know the way, and can make the ride in the dark."

"All right," he said, "but when you get there, tell the sheriff what's going on."

"It'll be my pleasure, mister."

"Then go."

She started for the door.

"Wait," Clint said. "Is he telling me the truth about this not being a working ranch? No ranch hands?"

"None except Sam," she said. "He sent his other men to help Harwick."

"Okay," he said, "you can go."

She ran to him, kissed his cheek, and said, "My name's Molly Sims. When you get to town, come to Molly's Café. You'll eat free."

"I'll be there."

She left, and he turned to Brock, who was securely tied to his chair.

"Pleasant dreams," he said.

In the morning Clint was waiting on the porch with a trussed-up Brock.

"Well," he said, "no sign of your loot."

"They'll be here," Brock said, "and you'll be outnumbered."

But when they heard horses, it was the sheriff from Flint, with a posse.

"You Clint Adams?"

"That's right."

The sheriff dismounted and shook hands with Clint. He was a tall man in his forties. His posse looked to be made up of deputies and townsmen, a full dozen.

"Sheriff Jeff Stone," he said. "Molly rode in and told us what happened."

"Brock thinks his men will be along with their loot," Clint said.

"Maybe, maybe not," Stone said. "Either way we'll find them and get it all back. Most of the people of Medicine Bow are still in Flint, waiting to return home."

"Does that include the Pattersons?"

"Yep, they're there."

"Their daughter is alive and should be in Givens right now, with a woman named Kathy."

"We heard from the sheriff of Givens," Stone said. "He's on his way with a posse of his own. Those looters can't move very fast with all that stuff. We'll catch him—but the one we really want is Dr. Brock." "I know, the whole thing was his idea." Clint looked over at the still trussed-up man.

"You don't know the half of it," Stone said. "Molly told us she overheard him planning the whole thing with his men. Brock gave those people a poison."

"What?"

"He created a phony epidemic to get them all to leave so he could loot the town."

"He killed twenty-seven people for that?"

"And more," Stone said, disgusted. "A lot of them were buried before the others left. He started out giving a few of his patients what he called a health tonic, then when they got sick, he told everyone else to come in and get some medicine to help fight off the disease. Instead it made them sick, too. After a bunch of them died, he changed the amount of poison so some folks would get better, but he got what he wanted—the rest of the town ran away. Of course, he didn't give it to his men, so they didn't get sick at all."

Clint turned, his hand twitching as he looked at Brock.

"I know what you're thinking, Adams," the lawman said. "If you did it, I'd like to give you a medal, but I'd have to arrest you. Just leave him to the law."

"He better hang," Clint said, "because if he doesn't . . ."

"If he doesn't," Sheriff Stone said, "I promise to look the other way."

Watch for

LOUISIANA STALKER

384TH novel in the exciting GUNSMITH series
from Jove

Coming in December!